"There's only one woman I've wanted as much as I want you right now—and she was scarcely a woman all those years ago."

Jenessa smiled, a slow, secret smile. "You mean me?"

"You don't need to ask." He lifted her hand to his lips, kissing her fingertips one by one.

For a moment sheer terror gripped her throat. As desire was inexorably replaced by anxiety, her nerves tightened to an unbearable pitch. In a very short time Bryce would know that she hadn't made love with anyone in the years since she'd ended up in his bed. That she was, at age twenty-nine, that anomaly—a virgin. And what would he conclude?

D0018872

This book is Part Two in an exciting new duet

MILLIONAIRE
MARRIAGES

from talented Harlequin Presents® author

Sandra Field!

In Book One,
The Millionaire's Marriage Demand (#2395),
you met Travis Strathern and Julie Renshaw—
and bore witness to the explosive chemistry
between them, which had dramatic consequences!

And here is Book Two,
The Tycoon's Virgin Bride:
Travis's sister Jenessa Strathern once had a
mammoth crush on Travis's best friend,
Bryce Laribee. Now, years later, she meets
Bryce again—and this time the
attraction is mutual!

Available only from Harlequin Presents®

Sandra Field

THE TYCOON'S VIRGIN BRIDE

MILLIONAIRE MARRIAGES

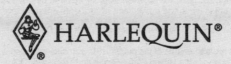

HARLEQUIN®

TORONTO • NEW YORK • LONDON
AMSTERDAM • PARIS • SYDNEY • HAMBURG
STOCKHOLM • ATHENS • TOKYO • MILAN • MADRID
PRAGUE • WARSAW • BUDAPEST • AUCKLAND

ISBN 0-373-12401-5

THE TYCOON'S VIRGIN BRIDE

First North American Publication 2004.

CHAPTER ONE

THE ridiculous thing was—so Jenessa Strathern decided afterward—that she had no sense of premonition when the telephone rang around seven o'clock on that sunny May evening. Nothing warned her to ignore the ringing, or told her to run outdoors and hide her head among the hydrangeas.

So much for feminine intuition.

She'd just stopped work, because the light was fading and she was so close to finishing this painting that she didn't want to risk any mistakes. Scrubbing a dab of alizarin crimson from her fingers with a stained rag, she picked up the receiver. "Hello?"

"Hi, Jen," her brother said. "Got a minute?"

She smiled into the receiver, plunking herself down in the nearest chair.

Travis Strathern, older than she by six years, lived in Maine with his wife, Julie, and their three-week-old daughter, Samantha. "For you," she said, "all the time in the world. How are you? Or I should say, how's Samantha?"

"Are you suggesting I've been usurped?"

"Samantha's cuter than you."

"I can't argue with that. Guess what? She can smile and hold on to my finger all by herself. Amazing, huh?"

Travis was a doctor who had a great many letters after his name and was highly qualified in tropical diseases. "Amazing," Jenessa said solemnly.

"She's the reason I'm calling. She's going to be christened in three weeks, and we'd like you to come. More than that, we'd like you to be her godmother."

5

Touched, Jenessa said, "That's sweet of you, Travis. But you do realize I'm a total dunce when it comes to babies? When you passed her to me in the hospital, I couldn't wait to pass her back—I was terrified I'd drop her."

"You'll learn," Travis said. "Anyway, she won't stay a baby for long. So you'll come?"

Jenessa hesitated. "Where's the christening taking place?"

"I knew you'd ask," Travis said wryly. "On Manatuck, at Dad and Corinne's. Do come, though, Jen...it's time you and Dad buried the hatchet, wouldn't you say? Especially now there's another generation in the picture."

She should say yes. She really should. It would hurt Travis's feelings if she didn't. As a child, she'd hero-worshiped her big brother, and as adult she both loved and respected him. Besides, she owed him a great deal, and although she hadn't seen a lot of Julie, she genuinely liked her. Julie had nearly lost Samantha in the fourth month of pregnancy; as a result, she and Travis had delayed a posting to Mexico until after the birth. So Samantha, Jenessa knew, was doubly precious to both of them.

So what if the christening was on Manatuck Island? She could surely behave in a civil fashion to Charles Strathern for a few hours, no matter that she normally avoided him like the plague.

But as Jenessa opened her mouth to accept the invitation, her brother added, "There's another reason I want you to come. We've asked Bryce to be Samantha's godfather...you know who I mean, Bryce Laribee, my old school friend?"

The color fled from Jenessa's cheeks and her heart began to thud as though a mallet was banging against her ribs. She made an indeterminate noise, her cold fingers clenched around the smooth plastic of the receiver. Oblivious to her reaction, Travis went on, "I don't think you've ever met him. Although that's hard to believe—I've known him since I was twelve. But now's your chance. He's a great guy, you'll like him."

Travis was wrong: Jenessa had met Bryce. Once, many years ago. And the feelings she'd had for him could scarcely be called liking.

She wasn't about to tell her brother that, however. Some secrets were better kept, her lovemaking with Bryce Laribee being right up there at the top of the list. The only trouble with secrets, she now thought unhappily, is that they brought deception in their wake. She had no intention of ever finding herself within ten miles of Bryce again; but she couldn't tell her brother that, either.

"Jen? Are you there?"

Frantically she tried to gather her wits. She had to get out of this somehow, which meant she'd have to stretch the truth. Considerably. What other choice did she have? She said, doing her best to sound convincing, "Travis, I'm sorry...but I can't take the time. It's a long drive all the way up to Maine from here, and I have a show opening in Boston early in July. At the Morden Gallery, so you know what that means."

"The Morden? Good for you—you're really going places."

She wasn't so sure about that. Knowing this was no time to enter a discussion about artistic stagnation, Jenessa said, "I'm behind schedule—they want twenty paintings by the end of June. If I come to Maine, it'll blow three or four days, and I just can't afford that kind of time."

There was a silence at the other end of the line. Then Travis said in a voice Jenessa had only rarely heard him use, "Are you being straight with me, sis? Are you sure the real reason isn't Charles? You know I'd understand if it were—he wasn't what you'd call an ideal father."

"I'm sure," she said, glad she could, if only briefly, speak the truth. "This show is important for me—I'm on the brink of making some sort of name for myself. The alternative is to sink into oblivion, and I've worked too hard the last twelve years to risk that.''

She'd met Bryce twelve years ago, in her first year at Columbia's School of the Arts, she thought with a sudden shiver. She'd been seventeen at the time.

With the ease of long practice, she closed her mind to that long-ago meeting with its lasting consequences. "I'm so sorry. But you know I'm devoted to Samantha, and that's what really counts, isn't it?''

"Julie's going to be disappointed.''

"So are you, by the sound of it.''

"Yeah...you didn't make it to our wedding, either.''

At which Bryce had been best man. Cursing the day she'd seen the poster advertising Bryce's lecture at Columbia all those years ago, Jenessa said, "Once the show's over, I promise I'll come for a visit. If you're both still speaking to me, that is.''

"Come off it,'' Travis said, "you know we're not like that. Tell you what—why don't you let me pay for your airfare? That way you could do the whole trip in a day.''

"I owe you too much money as it is...I don't want to go any deeper in debt.''

"A gift, Jen. No strings attached.''

"I can't take any more money from you, Travis—I just can't.''

There was another pregnant silence. Then her brother said, "You'll have to accept the title of godmother-in-absentia, then. Because we don't want anyone else but you.''

Tears pricked at Jenessa's lids. Her mother had run away to France when she had been just a baby, and from the time she was little, her father had done his best to crush any wayward impulses in his only daughter. Simultaneously, he'd blatantly favored her twin brother, Brent. To this day, she and Brent were as distant as it was possible for twins to be. Travis had been the one who'd been her rock as she grew up, despite his long absences at boarding school. To disappoint him now, hurt her deeply.

But she'd been utterly humiliated by Bryce in his hotel room in Manhattan; how could she possibly face him again?

She couldn't. It was out of the question.

She said valiantly, "How much does Samantha weigh? And is Julie getting enough sleep?"

Travis was happy to talk at some length about his daughter and his wife, both of whom he openly adored. In return, Jenessa described the new contract she had with her gallery, and the progress of her garden; finally, to her relief, Travis rang off. Slowly she put down the phone.

Once again she'd sidestepped any chance of coming face-to-face with Bryce Laribee. But the cost had been high; deep within her, Jenessa felt the slow burn of anger.

Against Bryce? Or against the young woman she'd been twelve years ago, so impressionable and so frighteningly vulnerable?

Late the following afternoon, Jenessa was down on her hands and knees in the vegetable garden. Tucked behind her tiny Quaker house, it was a peaceful spot, bathed in sunlight and alive with bees. A breeze whispered through the tall maples that bordered her property.

She'd finished the painting that morning. It was technically accomplished, as was all her work, its sunlit details overlying the sense of menace that haunted everything she painted.

She'd slept badly, dreaming of babies crying out from the high cliffs of Manatuck, and of her brother turning his back on her in an empty art gallery. And, of course, she'd dreamed of Bryce.

If only she'd never seen that poster on the bulletin board in the School of Arts...

* * *

His name jumped out at her first: Bryce Laribee. Best friend of her beloved brother, millionaire computer whiz. The title of his lecture was incomprehensible to her, although she did gather it had something to do with programming. It was his photograph in the top corner of the poster that held her skewered to the spot. Thick blond hair, gray eyes that looked right through her, a forceful bone structure that made her itch to draw his cleft chin, strong jaw and wide cheekbones.

An unapproachable face that drew her like a magnet.

Her artist's soul, fledgling though it was, knew she had to see him in person. Perhaps the photo lied. Perhaps when she saw him, she'd realize his face was nothing out of the ordinary, and there was no reason for this overwhelming urge to sketch him.

A portrait, she thought with a surge of excitement. Head and shoulders. In oils. Although she was new to portraiture, she was almost sure she could do him justice.

Realizing she'd been gazing at the poster like a starstruck groupie, Jenessa hurried off to her watercolor class. Telling none of her friends, the next evening she went to the lecture, sitting well at the back where she could see Bryce Laribee without being seen. He was standing full in the light on the auditorium stage; in the flesh, he far exceeded the promise of the photograph.

She had to sketch him. She had to.

But more than his features drew her. His rich baritone sent shivers up and down her spine, his sense of humor made her laugh, while his lucid descriptions almost made her understand what he was talking about. There was a reception in the department lounge after the lecture. She went, again tucking herself in the background, waiting until the crowd thinned to make her move. She'd decided on her first sight of him that she wasn't going to tell him she was Travis's sister; he was more than capable of subtracting six years from her brother's age and coming up with seventeen. If he knew she was that young, he'd never take her seriously. Game over before it began.

Bryce had approached the bar for another drink. She walked up to him, her heart racketing in her rib cage, and said with assumed calm, "My name is Jan Struthers, I'm an art student. I'm wondering if I could buy you a drink after this is over—I'd like to sketch you."

He looked her up and down, his gray eyes just as unrevealing as she'd expected: deep-set gray eyes over cheekbones hewn with potent masculinity. She swallowed hard. Wasn't his physical charisma exactly why she wanted to paint him? She couldn't back down now. That would be cowardly, and she'd never thought of herself as a coward.

His survey of her was leisurely; her heartbeat accelerated. She knew what he'd see: her spiky hair, its tips dyed bright orange, her elaborate makeup, contacts that made her eyes almost purple, and an outlandish beaded leather outfit that more than hinted at a sexuality she wasn't quite ready to acknowledge. For the first time, she found herself regretting she'd succumbed to the peer pressure of the other art students with their outrageous outfits; that her father would be appalled by her getup wasn't much help.

She should have toned herself down for this all-important meeting with Bryce Laribee.

As if proving her point, Bryce wasn't bothering to hide his amusement. "You're quite a creation. A work of art in itself."

Jenessa looked pointedly at his tailored business suit and impeccable tie. "You have your uniform, and I mine."

"Yours is more fun."

"Either way, they're what we hide behind."

"So we're basically the same underneath?"

She bit her lip, not sure what he was implying. "I didn't say that."

"And just what part of me did you want to sketch, Jan Struthers?"

She flushed; simultaneously, anger flickered to life. He was playing with her, cat to mouse. She could have told the truth: a head and shoulders portrait. Instead she said, "A good artist never narrows her options before she begins."

"She stays open to all the possibilities?"

"Of course."

The sparks in his eyes made her feel weak at the knees. Virgin though she was—a rarity among her classmates—there was no mistaking that he was flirting with her.

Flirting? Or was he putting the moves on her?

He couldn't be. She was being overly sensitive to innuendo.

He said, "I have to say goodbye to the organizers of the lecture...do you mind waiting for a few minutes?"

"I'll sharpen my pencils," she said demurely.

He laughed, his white teeth flashing, his whole face alive with a masculine energy that shuddered along her nerves. "I'll be as quick as I can," he said, and strode across the room toward a couple of tweed-jacketed professors.

Jenessa tossed back the last of her glass of wine. She'd suggest they go to a restaurant for coffee, or to a bar, where there'd be other people. She'd be quite safe.

She didn't feel safe. She could recall every detail of Bryce's face: the dark flecks in his irises, the determination in his jaw, the sensuality of his strongly carved mouth. He was a big man, towering over her, making her feel small and feminine. Oh, God, she thought helplessly, what was going on?

Then Bryce crossed the room toward her, and in a rush of adrenaline she knew she should have run for her life. Safe? Anywhere in his vicinity? Nothing about him was remotely safe. She was way out of her league.

But Jenessa, only a few months ago, had run away from

home, obeying every instinct of body and soul that had urged her to forge her own destiny. Why should she play it safe now? Art was about risks, and how could she take risks on a square of canvas if she never took them in her personal life? Doing her best to look cool and sophisticated, she asked, "Are you ready?"

"I have a rented car outside. Let's go."

She glanced down at her attire. "You don't care if they see you leaving with me?"

He raised his brows. "I don't live by anyone else's rules—maybe you should know that about me." He took her by the elbow, the warmth of his fingers on her bare skin sending ripples of heat through her body.

"Where are we going?" she faltered. "A bar would be fine, providing it's not too dark for me to see what I'm doing."

"Oh," he said deliberately, "I thought we'd go to my hotel. That way we won't be disturbed."

"I want to sketch you—that's all!"

"Is it? Is it really, Jan Struthers?"

They'd left the auditorium; the corridor was deserted. Lifting his hand, Bryce traced the softness of her lips with tantalizing slowness, his fingers lingering on the silky skin of her cheek. As her eyes widened, every nerve in her body sprang to life. She swayed toward him, her heart pounding in her breast. He said softly, "Underneath all that war paint, you're quite astonishingly beautiful."

He meant it, she realized dazedly. And already this had gone far beyond flirting. He wanted her. He, Bryce Laribee, self-made millionaire, wanted her, Jenessa Strathern, seventeen-year-old virgin.

Run for your life, Jenessa.

He was pressing the elevator button for the car park. She gasped, "I left my sketch pad at the studio by mistake. I—"

He laughed. "It was a novel approach, I must admit."

So all along he'd thought she was lying about her desire

to sketch him...how dare he? Dragging her attention back to what he was saying, she tried to focus. "So tell me about yourself, Jan—what brought you to Columbia? It's a fine school, so you must be talented. Should I be looking out for your name in a few years?"

He'd look a long time because her name was false. With a passion that surprised her, Jenessa said, "I don't want to follow the latest trend—which is always in reaction to the trend before it. I'm not using the word fad, but it might well apply. I want to paint what's true to me. Follow my instincts, my gut. No matter if it's unfashionable and doesn't fly." Abruptly she fell silent, wishing she'd kept her mouth shut.

"Interesting," he said. "Do you run your love life on the same principles?"

She had no love life. Had never really contemplated the possibility before this fraught meeting with her brother's best friend.

Bryce was standing altogether too close to her in the elevator, and like a shock of cold water she wondered if all along she'd been deceiving herself about her motives for meeting Bryce, out of simple ignorance of the forces that could ignite between a man and a woman. Had it been an artistic need? Or a sexual one? Or a blend of both? Her mouth dry, she blurted the truth. "I think I wanted you the minute I saw your photo on the poster."

"I'm a very rich man," he remarked.

With a shocked gasp Jenessa moved away from him, her back pressing into the wall. "I'm not after your money! I couldn't care less about it."

Narrow-eyed, he stared at her in silence for a full five seconds. "You mean that, don't you?"

The elevator doors slid open. She stayed where she was. "Yes, I do."

Bryce took her by the elbow, jamming his foot against the door. "You'd be surprised how many women look right through me and see nothing but my net worth."

She wasn't quite ready to surrender. "I'm not one of them."

"Then I apologize."

"Do you?" Jenessa flashed. "Really? Or are you just mouthing the words?"

"We're holding up the elevator," he said irritably. "This is a one-night stand, we're not talking marriage for life. So what does it matter?"

A one-night stand. How cheap that sounded. "I'm not going anywhere with you," she flared. "I really did want to sketch you—it wasn't a come-on."

"Look, I've apologized." He tugged her out of the elevator. "What more do you want?"

Anger had hardened his jawline; his energy, fierce and unyielding, called up a matching response in her from a place she refused to deny. "I don't like being called a liar."

"I'm taking your words at face value—that you're not interested in my money. Isn't that enough for you?"

"I guess it'll have to be," she retorted, her cheeks hot with temper.

With sudden impatience Bryce put his arms around her, pulled her to the length of his body and kissed her. His hunger, ruthless and imperious, wiped out her anger as if it had never been, replacing it with a surge of primitive passion that was utterly new to her. Drowning in it, she clung to him with all her strength. His hold tightened. Then she felt the first thrust of his tongue like the lick of fire. Instinctively molding her body to his, she opened to him; and in a rush of mingled amazement and pleasure realized that what he was demanding she was more than willing to give.

Abruptly Bryce released her, saying roughly, "The car's just outside. Let's go."

Jenessa stumbled after him, knowing that in one brief kiss she'd learned more about the power of one man's body over her own than she could have imagined. Enthralled. Swept off her feet. Bewitched. In a way that even ten minutes ago she couldn't have anticipated.

Bryce ushered her into the passenger seat of a silver Mercedes, and without a word drove out of the lot. Soon he was navigating the noisy streets, weaving in and out of the traffic. As though there'd been no hiatus in their conversation, he said, "There's something you should know about me. I fly to the west coast tomorrow and leave for Singapore the next day. I don't do commitment and I always use protection."

Something in his tone angered Jenessa profoundly. "Are you being purposely unromantic?"

"I'm telling you the way it is. If you don't like it, it's not too late to back out...I'll buy you a drink and no hard feelings."

Inadvertently he'd given her an excuse to escape from a situation that was way beyond her depth. She should take it, take it and run. It was perfectly clear to her that she'd never even have gotten into his car had he not been Travis's friend, and thus known to her by hearsay.

But then she remembered the incredible power of that single kiss; mysteriously, hadn't it transformed her into a woman truly aware of her own femininity? Was she going to run away from that?

With a barely discernible quiver in her voice, Jenessa said mendaciously, "My first rule is protection."

"Fine. And your second?"

This time she was telling the hard truth. "That no one, but no one, controls my life but me."

"Then we're on the same wavelength," Bryce said.

Jenessa sat back, trying to still the trembling of her limbs. Right now she was going on the assumption she'd have at least some control over whatever happened in Bryce's hotel room.

But what if she was wrong? What then?

CHAPTER TWO

As a CABDRIVER blared his horn, Jenessa gave a nervous start. She depended deeply on her intuition in the studio; it was now screaming that the next few hours could unalterably change her life in ways far more significant than any lost virginity.

She was under no illusions: she was about to go to bed with her brother's best friend. It was a crazy plan. Plain crazy. But never before had her blood fueled her body with such an undeniable and imperative ache of desire.

She'd allow herself to be seduced by Bryce; and then she'd leave. If he ever found out who she was, she was sure he'd never tell Travis.

In that, at least, she was quite safe. And how much better to lose her virginity with an experienced man who was, however obliquely, known to her, than to any of the fumbling undergraduates who had only filled her distaste. She said coolly, "I'll take a cab home afterward."

Not taking his eyes off the constant traffic, Bryce asked, "How old are you, Jan?"

Her lashes flickered. "Twenty-one."

"Do you graduate next spring?"

"No...I was late applying."

He said in exasperation, "I can't read you—you elude me. Usually women are an open book to me. But not you."

"Perhaps open books aren't worth reading." She gave a sudden chuckle. "Which sounds like a Japanese koan, doesn't it?"

"Mysterious? Paradoxical? You're both." He gri-

17

maced. "I'll be back in New York in a couple of months. Will you give me your phone number?"

"No."

Her answer, like everything else she'd done in the last hour, had been instinctive. Bryce said flatly, "You really are into control."

Suddenly exhilarated as much by their verbal fencing as by his physical presence, Jenessa said provocatively, "Is there any reason why I shouldn't be?"

Deliberately he took his hand from the wheel and slid it up her stockinged thigh, bared by her miniskirt. "I hope neither of us regrets this."

"There's no reason why either of us should," she said, as much to herself as to him; and made no attempt to hide her shiver of response.

Leaving his hand heavy and warm on her thigh, he said, "Two more blocks."

Ten minutes later, Bryce was ushering her through the double doors of the penthouse suite in one of the city's most prestigious hotels. She gained a quick impression of gleaming parquet and opulent Chinese carpets before Bryce said with the underlying impatience she was already realizing was characteristic of him, "Do you want anything to eat? Or drink?"

The courage that had preserved her time and again in her childhood came to the fore. She slipped her feet out of her shoes and stood on tiptoe to kiss him. "You and you," she whispered.

With a strength that intoxicated her, he lifted her in his arms and carried her the width of a richly furnished living room, its tall windows jeweled with the lights of the city. His corded muscles were hard against her body; she could hear the heavy pounding of his heart, an intimacy that made her faint with longing. He pushed the bedroom door open, strode across a thick carpet to the bed and lowered her onto it. Then he straightened and yanked at the knot of his tie.

Mesmerized, Jenessa watched as he hauled off his jacket, tie and shirt. He kicked his shoes to one side. Socks and trousers followed. His watch, whose price tag would probably have paid her entire year's tuition, he placed on the bedside table. Then, wearing only a pair of dark boxer shorts, he said softly, "Take off your clothes, Jan."

Jan, she thought. *Jan.* Another woman, a fictional woman. When all she wanted was to be herself.

She sat up, unzipping her black jacket. Her brief camisole, skintight, joined his clothes on the floor. Her bra was also black. She eased out of her skirt and drew her stockings slowly down her legs, her eyes glued to his face; scarcely able to breathe, she murmured, "I want you to take off the rest."

For a moment his gaze roamed the pale curves of her body. "You're so beautiful," he said huskily.

Wondering if she could die of waiting, Jenessa opened her arms to him. He plummeted to the bed, enveloping her in the heat of his body, flicking open the clasp of her bra and tossing it to the floor. Her breasts were firm, delicately pointed. With his tongue he found the soft peak, hardening it within seconds. Jenessa gave a startled gasp of pleasure, her body arching toward him. He circled her waist, lifting her so that they fitted together as though made for each other.

Against her pelvis she felt the hardness that was his essence: proof of his desire. Then he was kissing her, plundering her mouth for all its sweetness, his hands roaming her body. She tangled her fingers in the hair that curled on his chest, wanting to delay an exploration that melted every nerve she possessed, yet driven toward a completion she could only imagine.

Glorying in her nudity, she pressed thigh to thigh, hip to hip. He sank lower, his lips tracing the swell of her breasts, the sweet concavity of her navel and belly. Then he opened her legs, plunging to find all her sensitivities.

She cried out his name, writhing beneath him, losing herself in rhythms that were sheer delight.

With a muttered exclamation, Bryce reached for the small envelope by the bed. "Wait for me," he said roughly, "I want us to come together."

She had been waiting for him for months, ever since she'd fled the house where she'd grown up, she thought dazedly; waiting for a lover capable of unleashing a passion she hadn't known was hers. As she opened her thighs, he thrust between them, brushing her breasts with the hard wall of his chest.

Then she felt resistance, a sudden shaft of pain; despite herself, she flinched. With a suddenness that shocked her, Bryce pulled back. He said sharply, "Jan—you're a virgin."

"Yes. But I want you so much, I don't care if—"

He was holding his weight on his palms, his elbows taut; he looked appalled. "You've never done this before?"

"No...so what? What difference does it make?"

He said, each word falling like a stone on the bed, "You told me you were experienced."

"I didn't!"

"Not in so many words. But that's the impression you gave me. I don't have one-night stands with virgins, Jan Struthers. It's not my style. I want a woman who knows the score."

There was a sharp pain in Jenessa's belly; her skin was suddenly so cold that she was shivering like a half-drowned kitten. "You wanted me, you can't deny that. Experienced or not, you wanted me."

"I'm glad you put it in the past tense," he said savagely.

She wrapped her fingers around his arm. "Please, Bryce, don't stop now...I've waited all term to meet someone like you, someone who brings me to life and makes me realize why I'm made the way I am. I want you to be the first to make love to me. Please.''

He picked up her fingers and removed them from his arm, as though her touch disgusted him. Then he rolled off the bed, the hall light falling smoothly over the planes of his back. Picking up his clothes, he said, ''Get dressed. I'll drive you home.''

His muscles flowing like those of a jungle cat, he walked toward the bathroom. The door closed behind him with a decisive snap. Slowly Jenessa sat up.

It was over. He no longer wanted her.

With a whimper of distress she grabbed her scattered garments and pulled them on, her fingers trembling with haste. Her lacy underwear mocked her, as did her tight sweater and minuscule leather skirt. As a lover, she was a failure. As a woman, laughable.

She was fumbling with the zipper on her skirt when Bryce marched back into the bedroom, fully dressed. He said with cold precision, ''So what was this really about? Were you planning a little blackmail? Well-known tycoon rapes virgin?''

She paled, her eyes huge. He was like Charles, she thought, misjudging her totally, always assuming the worst. Were all men like that? All except her brother, Travis: who was, of course, Bryce's best friend.

What was she going to do next? Collapse in tears? Or call upon the pride that had been her salvation for the last many years?

She wasn't going to cry in front of Bryce Laribee. That much she knew. Standing tall, Jenessa spat, ''Don't judge me by the standards of your other women!''

''Then what did you do this for?''

''If you don't understand, there's no point in me trying to explain,'' she snapped, thrusting her arms into her jacket. ''I'll get a cab and you'll never hear from me again. Goodbye, Bryce. It's been instructive.''

''It certainly has. How old *are* you?''

She raised her chin, glaring at him. "Seventeen," she said. "But still old enough to know better."

"*Seventeen?*"

"That's what I said."

"And I believed every word you told me...you should be studying drama, not art."

She said flatly, "If you think I'm going to stand here half the night while you insult me, you couldn't be more wrong. Get out of my way."

He seized her by the elbow. "I said I'd drive you home."

"The only way you'll do that is with me kicking and screaming every inch of the way—is that what you want?"

"You little hellcat," he said with reluctant admiration, "you would, wouldn't you? Have you got enough money for a cab?"

She raised her chin another notch. "You're not the only person in the world with money."

"You're certainly behaving like some rich guy's spoiled brat."

He couldn't have said anything more calculated to hurt: *spoiled brat* had been one of the phrases her father used to fling at her when she was little. She said steadily, knowing she had to get out of here, "Stick to your own league, Bryce—women who don't challenge you."

"Don't tell me what to do," he said softly.

Fear trickled like ice water down her spine. Her mind blank, she walked past him out of the bedroom, all her nerves straining to hear if he would follow her. The living room seemed endless, the green carpet as vast as a football field. Then, finally, the penthouse door clicked shut behind her. The elevator arrived, she walked in and was carried down to the lobby. Chin still high, she crossed it and let the doorman hail her a cab. It wasn't until she got into her own little rented room in a very different area of town, the door latched and chained, that she allowed her pride to dissolve into tears of humiliation and pain.

Slowly Jenessa came back to the present. A hermit thrush was piping from the pines in her neighbor's lot, clear, silvery notes that brought an ache to her chest; she had, without even knowing what she was doing, weeded the entire row of green beans. Twelve years had passed since that evening, and yet her humiliating dismissal was as fresh as if it had happened yesterday. No wonder she couldn't bear the thought of going to Samantha's christening.

She got up, gathered the wilting weeds into her bucket and dumped them on the compost. The late May sun felt warm on her back; she should have put on shorts and a sleeveless top instead of her old gardening trousers and a baggy shirt.

Trying to shake off her mood, Jenessa looked around appreciatively. Her little peak-roofed house with its weathered, unpainted shingles and neat white trim, her tangled flower garden and tidy vegetable patch were where she belonged: haven and inspiration, the place where she could be herself. Five years ago, Travis had loaned her the money for the down payment; when she turned thirty, in a few months, she would receive her share of her grandfather's trust fund, and the place would really be hers.

She glanced at her watch. Another fifteen minutes weeding, then she'd head indoors and make something for supper.

Jenessa sank to her knees. Tomorrow she must start her next painting; she'd already done some sketches, although nothing about them had hardened into certainty. Idly the images began drifting through her mind, one after another, colors shifting and changing in the light...

"Excuse me," a man's voice said, "I'm looking for Jenessa Strathern."

That voice. That deep baritone voice. She'd have known it anywhere. And it was all too real: not part of her earlier reverie. The color draining from her face, Jenessa pushed herself upright and turned to face the intruder.

Bryce Laribee was standing on the garden path, not ten feet from her. He'd pushed dark glasses up into his sun-streaked blond hair; his eyes were still the unrevealing gray she remembered so well. Her throat dry, her cold palms pressed into her trousers, she croaked, "Who did you say?"

"I'm sorry," he said quizzically, "I didn't mean to startle you. I called out from behind the back porch, but you didn't hear me. I'm looking for Jenessa Strathern."

She hadn't heard because she'd just had a brain wave for the background of the painting. For a wild moment she contemplated lying to him, telling him she had no idea who Jenessa Strathern was or where he could find her. But Wellspring, the village in which she lived, was too small for her to hide. Any one of her neighbors would direct him back to the little Quaker house on the lane.

And then he'd know she'd been lying, and would wonder why.

She faltered, "I'm Jenessa. Who are you?"

He grinned down at her dirt-stained fingers. "I hope I won't insult you if I don't offer to shake hands. I'm Bryce Laribee, your brother Travis's friend."

Through a jumble of disconnected thoughts, Jenessa gave thanks that she was in her most disreputable clothes, her curls jammed under her straw hat, her face innocent of makeup. She couldn't look more different from the spike-haired, leather-clad siren she'd been at seventeen. "Oh," she said, "hello," and stretched her mouth in a smile that felt completely artificial.

He was wearing faded jeans and an open-necked checked shirt, the sleeves rolled up to the elbow. At his throat she saw his tangled body hair, on his arms blond hairs that caught the sun. As inevitably as one of her roses opening to the morning sun, desire blossomed in her belly, so impelling and ungovernable that she was terrified it would show in her face. She still wanted him, she thought with a sick lurch of her heart. Just as much as she had twelve years ago.

How could she?

Thank heavens for the dirt on her fingers; if he'd shaken her hand, she'd have been lost.

He said easily, "I can see I've interrupted you."

"Oh, no, that's all right," she stumbled. "I was going to stop soon anyway."

"You have a lovely spot here."

"Yes. I'm very lucky."

"Is there somewhere we can sit down? You've probably already guessed that Travis sent me."

She hadn't. Wiping her palms down her trousers, Jenessa indicated the wooden benches under the old apple tree. "We can sit there," she said. Not for anything was she going to invite him indoors.

The tree was still in bloom, the pink and white flowers delicately scenting the air. Petals had collected on the flagstones in drifts, like snowflakes. Jenessa sat down, the wood hard against her thighs. Think, Jenessa, she told herself. Think.

Bryce said pleasantly, "Travis phoned me last night after he'd spoken to you. Let me put my cards on the table. He's hoping I can persuade you to come to the christening—despite the fact that it's on Manatuck, and that your father, stepmother and mother will all be there."

At any other time, Jenessa might have been amused by Bryce's directness. She said with some semblance of spirit, "I told Travis I couldn't come because of the pressures of work."

Pointedly Bryce looked around the peaceful garden. "You don't look particularly pressured to me."

Her cheeks warmed with anger. "The reason I didn't

hear you calling me, Mr. Laribee, was because I was thinking about my next painting, which I have to start tomorrow morning. I have a major show in Boston in a few weeks, and I can't afford the time to travel up to Maine and back. It's that simple.''

"Travis told me about the show. You're doing well.''

"If I am, it's because I work hard. You're a businessman, aren't you? I'd have expected you to understand that.''

Bryce fished in his pocket and brought out a folded cheque. Holding it out, he said, "From Travis. To pay for your airfare.''

She kept her hands firmly at her sides. "I already told him I couldn't take any more money from him. I owe him too much as it is.''

"Then I'll pay your way.''

She raised her brows. "If I won't take money from my brother, I'm not likely to take it from a complete stranger.''

"I'm Travis's best friend. Scarcely a stranger.''

"This is about time, not money,'' Jenessa said, her voice rising. "Can't you understand that?''

"Okay, let's cut out the euphemisms,'' Bryce said evenly. "This discussion isn't really about a christening. It's about a whole lot more—you know that as much as I do.''

"I don't know what you're talking about.''

"Listen to me,'' he said grimly, "and you will. Travis is your brother, he's been very good to you over the years, and he loves you. You didn't bother going to his wedding…God knows why. Surely you can understand how much Julie means to him, how important that ceremony was to both of them. Besides, Julie wants to get to know you. She's a real sweetheart and deserves a lot better than being ignored.''

Jenessa hadn't gone to the wedding because Bryce had

been best man. "This isn't about Travis. It's about Charles and—"

"All right, so you don't get along with your dad, your stepmother or your mother. Not one of them. But to stay away from Travis's wedding because you can't be civil to your family for the space of one day doesn't wash with me. And now you're doing the same thing all over again. Although this time you're using your painting as an excuse. Your painting and money."

"I have to earn my living," Jenessa put in hotly.

But Bryce overrode her. "Julie nearly lost Samantha midway through her pregnancy—I'm sure you're aware of that. So that little baby is the apple of their eye. They dote on her, they adore her...and now they've asked you to be her godmother. But do you care? No, ma'am. You can't even spare a day to fly up there."

Put like that, it sounded horribly selfish; no wonder Bryce couldn't condone her behavior. Knowing she was probably only going to dig herself deeper into trouble, Jenessa said weakly, "Of course I know how much they love Samantha. But the timing's as bad as it could be. A show at the Morden is a huge accolade, I can't afford to play around right now."

His jaw hardened. "The message I'm getting is that you're totally self-absorbed. It doesn't matter that your brother loves you and his wife wants to get to know you, and that by inviting you to be Samantha's godmother they're asking you to be an important part of their lives. You've shut yourself up in an ivory tower called art. And you're far too pure-minded to descend to the level of ordinary people."

With a gasp of pure rage Jenessa said, "What gives you the right to speak to me like this?"

"My friendship with Travis does. You say you owe him money. Well, I owe him my life," Bryce announced in a voice like a steel blade. "If it wasn't for him, I'd be on the streets, in jail or dead."

He broke off so abruptly that Jenessa said flatly, "You didn't mean to tell me that."

"You don't deserve any information about my private life."

"It's wasted on me anyway," she said, not altogether truthfully. "My mind's made up."

"So I'm supposed to stand by and do nothing while you ignore what's most important to Travis—his wife and his child?"

"I'm afraid you'll have to. Because it's not your decision."

"Do you really think you can do exactly what you please without hurting their feelings? Because that's the bottom line, isn't it? You're disappointing both of them."

Unerringly Bryce had found her most vulnerable spot. "Once the show is over, I'll go and visit them," Jenessa said in a thin voice. "I told Travis I would. In the meantime, I'll thank you to mind your own business."

"Frankly, having met you, I have no idea why he bothers to keep in touch."

Jenessa stood up. "I'm sorry you came all this way for nothing, Mr. Laribee," she said tightly. "But you're wasting your time and mine as well."

"So that's your last word?"

"Yes."

"Fine. Then you'd better go back to thinking about your painting, hadn't you, Miss Strathern? I'll tell Travis that daubing oil on canvas is more important to you than celebrating family occasions. Although I bet he's already gotten that message."

Bryce turned on his heel and strode along the path, disappearing around the corner of the house. A few moments later, Jenessa heard the sound of a car engine accelerating down the lane. Then, once again, silence fell over the garden. The only sound she could hear, apart from the drone of insects, was the thick pounding of her own heart.

He'd gone. He hadn't recognized her. Hadn't connected Travis's sister with a young art student he'd gone to bed with many years ago, and then ruthlessly dismissed.

She sank back down on the bench, pulling her hat off and shaking out her mass of blond curls. Through the turmoil of emotion in her breast, one conclusion was clear: Travis must really want to see her to send his good friend Bryce to plead his cause.

Once again, she was disappointing her brother. Just as she had at his wedding.

Maybe she should tell Travis the truth, she thought, trying to ease some of the tension out of her shoulders. Confess what had happened—or rather, what hadn't happened—all those years ago between her and Bryce. Get it over with. Surely such a confession wouldn't damage his friendship with Bryce, not after this long. And it would put things straight between her and Travis, something she craved with all her heart.

But wouldn't Travis then connect her confession with the lack of suitors in her life, with her continued refusal to become involved with someone, or to get married? He'd assume she'd been in love with Bryce. That Bryce had repudiated a lot more than her body. She couldn't bear it if that happened. One humiliation was enough.

More than enough.

Jenessa staggered out of bed at eight-thirty the next morning. At two, three and four she'd been wide awake, staring into the darkness: her body craving the touch of the only man who'd ever swept her off her feet, her mind racing between a hotel room in New York City twelve years ago and her own garden the evening before. At three-thirty she'd gotten out of bed and gone to her studio, where she'd produced a series of very unsatisfactory sketches for her new work, tossed them aside and covered page after page with sketches of Bryce. Bryce in her garden, Bryce naked in the shadows of a luxurious bedroom, Bryce in her arms. These, too, she'd tossed aside. Finally, about five-thirty, she'd fallen into a dead and unrefreshing sleep that had mercifully been dreamless.

Coffee, she thought, yawning, stretching to get the aches out of her limbs. Coffee and a shower. Maybe then the day would seem worth beginning.

While the coffee dripped through the grinds, she wandered to the kitchen window. A sudden movement caught her eye. Her whole body stilled.

A man was hunkered down in the vegetable garden, weeding, his shirt stretched tight across the muscles of his back, the early sun glinting in his blond hair. He looked very much at home and completely at ease, and it was this that made Jenessa forget any vestige of caution. She slammed her empty mug down on the counter, marched through the mudroom and hauled the back door open. The hinges squealed. The man looked up.

CHAPTER THREE

THE sun was behind Bryce, shining full on the woman on the porch. She looked utterly magnificent, he thought, brushing the dirt from his hands. She also looked extremely angry.

Good. He was all too ready to take her on.

She ran down the board steps in her bare feet, her cream silk pajamas brushing the swell of her breasts and clinging to her thighs. Her hair was a wild tangle of curls, her eyes bluer than the sky and her cheeks the pink of the apple blossoms on the tree just behind him. To his dismay, his groin tightened involuntarily.

How could he desire a woman he so thoroughly disliked?

Was that one reason he was so angry with her? A reason that had nothing to do with Travis or Julie.

Standing up, he said cordially, "Good morning, Jenessa."

She stopped three feet away from him, her hands on her hips. "Just what do you think you're doing?"

"Weeding...isn't it obvious?"

She glanced downward. "Weeding?" she squeaked. "You've just pulled up three-quarters of the beet seedlings."

"You're kidding. You mean those funny little red-colored things would have turned into beets?"

"If you hadn't hauled them up by the roots, they would have!"

Realizing he was thoroughly enjoying himself, Bryce said, "You should have got up earlier...I thought you had

31

a painting to start. Then I wouldn't have done so much damage.''

''You should have gone back where you belong yesterday evening,'' she stormed. ''Why don't you head back there right now? Ten minutes ago wouldn't be too soon.''

''Boston's where I belong,'' he said. ''I decided I'd given up entirely too easily yesterday, so I stayed in a charming bed-and-breakfast down the road. Whose owner, by the way, gave me the lowdown on you—on the lack of men in your life, and on the peculiarities of modern art as exemplified by your paintings.''

''Wilma Lawson,'' Jenessa groaned, momentarily forgetting that she was in a rage.

''That's the one. Why aren't there any men in your life, Jenessa?''

''Because far too many men are just like you.''

He threw back his head and laughed. ''I'm not that bad.''

''Says who? And why is this discussion taking place at the level of a couple of seven-year-olds?''

''So I'll keep my mind off how enchanting you look in those pajamas,'' Bryce said promptly.

Hot color flooded her cheeks in a way that intrigued him. She was twenty-nine years old, he knew that from Travis. But she was blushing as though she were sixteen. As though she'd never been complimented by a man in her life.

Impossible. The way she looked, she must be surrounded by men. Day and night.

Not a thought he cared for.

He'd said she looked enchanting. He should have said sexy. Voluptuous. Seductive. He wanted to take her in his arms and kiss those delectable, sleep-swollen lips. Feel the warmth of her skin beneath the smooth silk. Run his hands through that tumbled mass of hair.

For Pete's sake, what was the matter with him? He'd come back here this morning to tell her she was going to

Maine come hell or high water. Not to seduce her. That wasn't on the cards. Apart from anything else, she was the kid sister of his best buddy.

Jenessa said in a strangled voice, "There aren't any men in my life in Wellspring. For one thing, most of the men here are over sixty. More to the point, half the village is made up of gossips like Wilma Lawson. So I keep my love life and my home life separate. One in Boston. One here. Okay?"

No, Bryce thought irritably, it wasn't okay. "Are you shacked up with anyone in Boston?"

"Are you?" she countered.

"Nope. No marriages, no divorces, no kids and no commitments."

So he hadn't changed, Jenessa thought, and to her intense annoyance found herself wondering why he'd never married. It was none of her business; he was nothing to her now. Nothing. She said crossly, "Why don't we get back on track? I'll repeat what I said yesterday—I can't come to Maine, not before my show. You can tell my brother you did your best. Goodbye, Bryce Laribee. Have a nice drive back to Boston. Have a nice life. But from now on, stay out of my hair."

Patently unimpressed, he remarked, "You blew it by not going to Travis's wedding—now you've got the chance to redeem yourself. Simple."

If only it were that simple. "Go away!" she exclaimed.

Closing the distance between them so that he was standing altogether too close, Bryce said lazily, "I can smell coffee. Aren't you going to offer me any?"

Six-foot-two, broad-shouldered and long-legged: none of that had changed, either. Elusively, the tang of his aftershave wafted to Jenessa's nostrils. Fighting to keep her hands at her sides so she wouldn't be tempted to run one finger down the cleft in his chin, she said, "I wasn't planning on it, no."

"I'm going to camp on your doorstep until you agree

to come to the christening. So you might as well get used to having me around.''

''I'll set the police chief on you!''

''Tom Lawson? First cousin of Wilma? I met him yesterday evening, told him I was here to see you, and that your brother and I were good friends. He seemed like a nice guy.''

Again Bryce had outwitted her. Jenessa took a long, slow breath. ''You really are insufferable.''

''Coffee, Jenessa.'' He indicated a paper bag on the bench under the apple tree. ''A couple of Wilma's Danish pastries—thought you might like one. They're stuffed with raspberries and custard. They'll go just fine with brewed Colombian.''

Jenessa stared up at him. Hadn't his determined jaw and strong bones enthralled her from the start? Clearly a lot more than his jaw was determined. He wasn't going to go away. And the longer he stuck around, the greater the chance he'd recognize her. Or that she'd fall on him like a sex-starved virgin, a prospect she couldn't bear to contemplate.

She'd be better to send him packing, turn up at the christening in her most elegant outfit and make sure on any subsequent visits to her brother that Bryce Laribee was conducting business on the opposite side of the globe. She said evenly, ''Okay. You win. I'll come to Maine. So you can leave right now. Mission accomplished.''

Something flickered in Bryce's eyes. ''It's not often a woman takes me by surprise,'' he said. ''Why the sudden capitulation?''

''Oddly enough,'' she said pleasantly, ''the thought of you camped on my front doorstep doesn't turn me on.''

''I don't turn you on. That's what you're saying.''

''You can interpret it any way you like.''

His voice deepened. ''We could put it to the test.''

She stepped back quickly, her deep blue eyes widening in what was unquestionably panic. ''Don't you dare!''

Bryce stood still, his brain racing. "What are you so frightened of?"

She bit her lip. "I'm not."

He said dryly, "If I really came on to you, you'd only have to scream and three-quarters of the village would come running. Including the police chief."

"And then they'd talk about nothing else for the next six months."

"So by kissing you, I'd be doing them a favor?"

Jenessa took another step back. "Bryce," she said edgily, "I'm hungry and I want my breakfast. Tell my brother I'll be there for the christening and that I'll pay my own way, and go back to Boston."

Bryce edged around her and picked up the paper bag. "Coffee first."

"I can see why nobody married you—you don't listen to one word anyone says," she flared, and marched away from him toward the house.

Her hips swung in her silk pajamas; her silky curls bounced between her shoulders. Bryce followed her, wishing he could ignore her as successfully as she was ignoring him.

Be honest, Bryce. You're not used to women turning their backs on you. You're used to them draping themselves all over you.

A change is as good as a rest? Yeah, right. And what in hell had made her change her mind?

The screen door banged in his face because Jenessa hadn't bothered holding it open for him. He let himself in, glancing around a small mudroom where jackets hung on hooks and boots were lined up on the floor. Then he walked into the kitchen.

There was no sign of Jenessa. But the coffee smelled delicious. By checking out the cupboards and refrigerator, he located two mugs, some cream and a sugar bowl, as well as plates for the pastries. A couple of minutes later, when Jenessa came into the room dressed in paint-stained jeans and a sweatshirt, her hair in an untidy cloud around her head, he was sitting at the table sipping his coffee.

"You sure know how to make yourself at home," she said.

"Bachelors fall into two classes. Those who want a woman to look after them and those who fend for themselves. Guess which kind I am?"

"There are some women, including me," she said pointedly, "who don't see their life's work as looking after a man."

"Congratulations," he said dryly.

After pouring herself a mug of coffee, Jenessa sat down across from him; her back was to the light. Cutting one of the pastries in half, she took a big bite and started to chew. "How can I stay mad at you when I've got a mouthful of raspberries and custard?" she mumbled. "Yum. Wilma's known across two counties for her baking. She sells homemade bread all year...it's my downfall."

A crumb was caught on her bottom lip. Unable to help himself, Bryce leaned forward and brushed it off, the softness of her mouth vibrating along his nerve ends. She shrank back, her jaw tense, her blue eyes full of fear. Frowning, he said, "You act like you're scared to death of me. Have you had a bad experience with a man?"

"So what if I have?"

"What did he do to you?" he demanded.

"Bryce, my past is none of your concern."

His gaze still fastened on her face, he said more moderately, "I'm sorry if I've done anything to frighten you, Jenessa. It certainly wasn't my intention."

For the first time, Jenessa felt a twinge of liking for him; and more than a twinge of guilt that she was deceiving him. "Apology accepted," she said through another mouthful of custard.

"Why don't you tell me about it?"

She drew in her breath sharply and choked on a crumb.

Quickly Bryce went to the sink, filled a glass with water and passed it to her, his fingers brushing hers. Ringless fingers, long and graceful, yet undeniably capable. Dark green paint was lodged under her nails. Frowning again, he said more to himself than to her, "You know, it's funny—every now and then you remind me of someone...the way you move, the shape of your face. But I can't remember who it is."

Jenessa buried her face in the glass, her pulse racing in her throat. Another ten minutes and he'd be gone. Then she'd be safe. Letting her hair fall forward, she cut another chunk of pastry. "My eyes are the same color as Travis's," she mumbled.

He laughed. "I ain't talking about a guy, baby."

"You've known so many women, I'm sure it's not easy to remember them all," she said waspishly.

For some reason wanting to set the record straight, Bryce announced, "From the time I was twenty until I turned twenty-five, I went through money, houses, cars and women as though there was an unending supply of each. But then all of a sudden it palled. Sure, I date sometimes, and I have the occasional affair. But nothing to get excited about."

"I can't imagine why you're telling me this."

Neither could he. "So how many men in Boston, Jenessa?"

He'd been honest with her: even if it had hurt something deep inside her to find out that all those years ago she'd simply been one in a long procession of women. Taking another gulp of coffee, Jenessa said flatly, "Men? None. At the moment."

"My home base is there. I'll leave you my phone number and address—next time you come into the city, we could have dinner."

She made a noncommittal noise. "I don't like driving back after dark. Bryce, if I don't get to work in the next five minutes, the gallery'll be firing me and I'll have no reason to go into Boston.''

He swallowed the last of his coffee and pushed back his chair. But instead of heading for the front door, he walked over to the doorway of her studio, his eyes wandering over its intriguing blend of chaos and extreme order, his nostrils registering the pungent odors of linseed oil and turpentine. Then his gaze sharpened. ''Is that the painting you just finished?''

With noticeable reluctance Jenessa said, ''Yes, it is.''

The scene she'd depicted could have been one of the streets where he'd grown up. She'd chosen a sunny summer evening, and had given loving attention to every detail; yet the boarded windows, piled-up garbage and rusted cars were infused with foreboding. He said harshly, ''How do you know what those streets are like?''

''I've walked through them.'' She hesitated. ''Travis told me you grew up in the slums of Boston.''

''Why did he tell you that?'' Bryce said in an ugly voice.

''It was only in passing. Nothing specific.''

''I don't talk specifics. Not to him or anyone else.''

She said gently, ''Maybe it's time you did.''

''Maybe it's not.'' His gaze shifted. ''Are those sketches for the new work?''

In a flurry of movement, Jenessa inserted her body between him and the untidy pile of papers. If he saw her drawings of his naked body, she'd die right on the spot. She gabbled, ''Nobody sees any work of mine until it's finished.''

''There,'' he said, ''you did it again, it's something about the way you move. Who the devil do you remind me of?''

''I have no idea! Bryce, please go, I've got work to do.''

He took a card out of his wallet and put it down on the table. ''Call me, Jenessa.'' Then his smile broke out, igniting his features with a purely masculine energy. "Travis will be very happy to see you at the christening."

If she told Bryce she'd changed her mind, he'd stay in Wellspring. If she went to the christening, she risked him remembering their long-ago encounter. Maybe in the next three weeks she'd come down with pneumonia. Or break a leg.

He held out his hand. "Someday you're going to tell me about the guy who made you so afraid. Then I'll go and punch him out for you."

If only he knew how ironic his offer was. Reluctantly Jenessa placed her hand in his, searingly aware of the latent strength of his grasp and the heat of his palm against hers. His grip tightened. Her heart banging against the cage of her ribs, she said evenly, "Goodbye, Bryce. Safe journey." Then she tugged her hand free.

She heard his footsteps cross the floorboards in the living room, and then the front screen squeak on its hinges. She should oil every door in the place, she thought. But house repairs never had been her strong point.

A minute or two later, Bryce's car drove away down the lane. Jenessa sagged against the studio door. For the space of three weeks she was safe.

It didn't feel like very long.

CHAPTER FOUR

BRYCE stepped off the launch onto the long wharf that jutted out from the island of Manatuck, where, money no object, Travis's father Charles had built a castle that wouldn't have been out of place in the Austrian alps. Bryce had seen the towers and turrets of Castlereigh before, and they had never failed to amuse him. Today, however, he had something other than castles on his mind.

Had Jenessa come to the christening as she'd promised? Would he discover when he saw her again that she was just another woman, beautiful of course, but nothing exceptional? Certainly nothing to warrant the way she'd been lodged in his mind the last three weeks. He'd spent one week in Brussels, and the last couple of days in Finland; the rest of the time he'd been home in his house on Beacon Hill. He'd thought about her in all three places far more than he was comfortable with.

She hadn't phoned. Not that he'd expected her to. Nor had he visited her, although he could have; she lived only an hour or so outside the city.

He strode up the slope, aware that he was probably the last guest to arrive; there'd been a delay unloading the luggage at the airport. Friends and family were gathered in the rose garden between the boathouse and the woods. The June weather had cooperated wonderfully, giving a clear sky with only a few scudding clouds. A light wind was laden with the scents of evergreens, of roses and the sea.

Then he saw Jenessa standing under a white-painted arbor, talking to Travis and Julie, and a spring that had

40

been tightly coiled inside his chest relaxed. She'd come. She'd kept her word.

Judging by his heart rate, he'd just rowed across the bay that separated Manatuck from the coastline of southern Maine, rather than standing peacefully on the deck of the launch. Dammit, Bryce thought. I don't need this. She's an uptight, unfriendly woman who's the sister of my best friend, and if I was smart I'd keep my distance. Big time.

What he really wanted to do was march past the roses, take her in his arms and kiss her senseless.

That'd really impress the guests. As for her reaction, he could think of several possibilities, all of them hazardous to his health.

"Hello, Bryce."

He dragged his eyes away from Jenessa and said with genuine pleasure, "Leonora, how are you?"

Leonora Connolly was the mother of Travis and the twins, Brent and Jenessa. Soon after the twins were born, she'd fled to Paris to pursue her career as an avant garde dancer. The reaction of her husband, Charles, had been to tell six-year-old Travis that she was dead; by dint of threats ensure that she never got in touch with any of her children; and then divorce her secretly. Two years after her departure, he'd married Corinne, a woman who couldn't have been more different from Leonora.

Last summer Leonora had traveled to Maine and had sought out her children. In the intervening months she and Travis had built a solid relationship; but according to Travis, Jenessa was indifferent to the sudden appearance of a mother she'd never known and had always assumed was dead.

"Another family gathering," Leonora said dryly. "I'm as well as could be expected."

"Under the circumstances, you look great."

She was tall and slim, her long black hair streaked with

gray, her every movement imbued with a dancer's grace. "So you're to be Samantha's godfather," she said.

"And Jenessa's the godmother," Bryce replied with a lift of his brow. "I met her for the first time three weeks ago. Talk about the original ice maiden."

"When I first saw Travis last summer, he was very angry with me for abandoning him when he was only six. In retrospect, I prefer his anger to the impeccable good manners with which Jenessa treats me. As though I was a chance-met stranger who means nothing to her."

"She's a very talented artist."

"You're right. I'd like to go to her opening at the Morden Gallery next month...will you be there?"

"I might."

"She's also exceptionally beautiful," Leonora said, a twinkle in her eye.

"I've wondered if that's why Travis asked me to go and visit her. Matchmaking. He ought to know better."

Leonora laughed. "Perhaps you should go and say hello to him. The ceremony's supposed to start in a few minutes."

"We'll talk again afterward," he promised, and headed toward Travis and Julie; but on the way, he was hailed by Brent Strathern, Jenessa's twin brother. "Hi there, Bryce, how's it going?" Brent said breezily.

Brent was handsome, charming and—in Bryce's opinion—spoiled rotten. "Fine. I'll be happier when I've done my thing with Samantha," he replied amiably.

Brent bared his teeth in a smile. "You're like me— you've had the sense never to get hitched."

Bryce didn't like being bracketed with Brent, who was known to be a womanizer and suspected of dubious financial dealings. He said mildly, "Your sister doesn't seem to have matrimony in mind, either."

"Jenessa? Who's she going to meet in a dump like Wellspring?"

"Artistically, it's not doing her any harm."

"Contemporary art's nothing but a big scam," Brent said edgily. "So she can slop paint on a canvas...big deal."

It was interesting, Bryce thought, that the privileged twin was jealous of the twin who'd been ignored by her father for years. "I suspect there's a little more to Jenessa's paintings than that," he said. "I guess I'd better say hello to my host and hostess...excuse me, Brent."

"See you later," Brent said.

Not if I can help it, thought Bryce, and strode between the rose beds toward Charles and Corinne.

Charles Strathern was tall and thin-haired, his handsome face underlaid by obstinacy rather than real strength. Corinne, as always, looked as serene and imperturbable as if she'd stepped out of the pages of a fashion magazine. However, her passion for roses was responsible for the beauty of their setting; Bryce had often thought there was more to Corinne than met the eye.

He shook Charles by the hand and kissed Corinne's cool cheek. "It's a real pleasure to be here," he said. "The garden's lovely, Corinne. And the weather couldn't be better."

"A very happy occasion," Charles said bluffly.

"She's a sweet baby," Corinne added. "The charm of being a grandparent, of course, is that you can hand your grandchild back to the parents whenever you like."

It was difficult to imagine Corinne dealing with a dirty diaper. Bryce kept this thought to himself, and answered Charles's queries about his latest travels. "So you and Jenessa are to be the godparents," Charles said. "I'm glad Jenessa came. She hasn't been to Manatuck for many years."

From Travis, Bryce already knew that Jenessa had no use for her father, whose main aim from the time she was little had been to crush her artistic impulses: impulses she'd presumably inherited from her runaway mother. "Then she's seeing it at its best," he said smoothly.

"She has a show opening next month in Boston," Charles labored on. "We thought we might attend."

Charles and Corinne owned a luxurious mansion in Back Bay, one of Boston's most prestigious addresses. "Jenessa could be on the brink of a highly successful career," Bryce said blandly.

"She graduated from Columbia's School of the Arts," Charles remarked. "A very fine school."

Bryce's heart gave a great jolt in his chest; the rose garden, the polite chatter of the assembly and the soft sighing of the waves vanished from his consciousness as if they no longer existed. "Columbia?" he rasped. "When?"

Not noticing Bryce's tone, Charles did some quick mental calculations. "She enrolled twelve years ago. So she must have graduated when she was twenty-one."

Twelve years ago Jenessa had been seventeen. The same age as the spike-haired art student who'd said she wanted to sketch him after that lecture he'd given at Columbia.

But the art student had had eyes that were almost purple.

Contacts, Bryce. Colored contacts.

The way Jenessa moved, the elegance of her lean, capable fingers, that elusive sense that somewhere he'd seen her before...his intuitions had been dead-on. He had.

In his bed. Twelve years ago.

Jan Struthers had been Jenessa Strathern. What a fool he'd been not to make the connection.

"Bryce, are you all right?" Corinne asked.

Hastily Bryce pulled himself together, furious that he'd revealed, if only partially, the shock of his discovery to Charles and Corinne. "Sorry, I was just wondering if I'd met her on a visit I made to Columbia some years ago," he said with a minimal degree of honesty.

Charles gave a hearty laugh. "Computers and art don't go together," he said, "so I rather doubt it. Bryce, I saw that article about you in the *Financial Times* recently, where they were explaining how extremely well you've done by maintaining your independence from any of the big corporations. You're to be congratulated, that's not an easy road.''

Talk about your career, Bryce. Talk about anything other than the fact that Jenessa Strathern, a woman you lust after, has already been in your bed. When she was still a teenager. ''That's high praise, Charles,'' he said wryly. ''But you know me—what other choice did I have? I'm far too single-minded, not to say stubborn, to work for someone else.''

It was true. He'd always been a loner; for many years it had suited him to go his own way, both in his business life and his personal life. ''But thanks for the compliment,'' he added. ''Now maybe I'd better go and say hello to the proud parents, and take a peek at Samantha. I only hope she doesn't cry when I pick her up.''

''If she does, pass her back to her mother,'' Corinne said with a mocking smile.

''Good advice,'' he grinned. Excusing himself, Bryce crossed a pebbled path and a stretch of manicured lawn toward the arbor. Through his long struggle to reach the international reputation Charles had applauded, he'd learned a number of lessons, the first of which had been to mask his feelings. Discouragement, ambition, anger, despair: he'd taught himself to hide them all. But could he dissemble the chaos of emotion in his chest right now from his best friend and from the woman who'd gone to his hotel room when she was only seventeen? He wasn't sure he could.

He'd soon find out. ''Hi Travis, Julie,'' he said. ''Hello, Jenessa.''

Travis clapped him on the shoulder, his black hair ruffled by the wind; in a time-honored ritual, Bryce punched Travis lightly on the chest. The two men were similar in height, and since sports were one of their shared interests, were both of athletic build. But there the similarities ended, for Travis's emotions, since he'd met Julie, were much more on the surface than those of his friend. *Open up, man,* Travis was apt to say to Bryce: with as much effect as if he'd addressed the walls of a squash court.

Julie gave Bryce a friendly kiss on the cheek, while Jenessa said in a voice as cool as the ocean, "Hello, Bryce."

She looked rather like the ocean, he thought, in her pale turquoise linen dress, her matching hat circled by a froth of white flowers. Her unruly curls framed her face; her makeup accentuated the elegance of her cheekbones and the depths of her eyes. Blue eyes. Not purple. Fathoms deep, and unfathomable.

Spurred by an anger he wasn't ready to acknowledge, he took her by the elbow and bent his head, kissing her on both cheeks, European fashion. Her body tensed at his touch. Her perfume was subtle, her skin smooth as silk and warm as the sun that lanced through the trees.

Kissing Jenessa wasn't remotely like kissing Julie. Not that he'd expected it to be. "How nice of you to come," he said, and watched fury bring an added flush to her already hectic cheeks.

A second realization thudded through his chest. Jenessa was no more immune to him now than she had been at Columbia. She'd wanted him then; and unless he was losing his marbles, she wanted him now. Was that why she'd been so afraid of him in her little house in Wellspring?

His anger increasing another notch, Bryce remembered how he'd offered to punch out the man who'd made her so afraid; and how she'd gone along with this story. But the whole time she must have been laughing at him behind his back.

It would give him great pleasure to find out if she still desired him. But not now. Later.

Glancing at her sister-in-law's high color, Julie said hastily, "Samantha's done nothing but sleep all day...we figure she's getting ready to scream her way through the ceremony.''

''Jenessa flew up last night,'' Travis added, ''so we've had a great visit. How was Helsinki?''

''Wet, dreary and profitable,'' Bryce said succinctly. ''When are you going back, Jenessa? I left my car at the wharf on the mainland, I could drive you to the airport.''

''Oh, no thanks,'' she said hastily. ''I arranged with Oliver for a drive later on today.''

Oliver was the captain of the launch that plied between Manatuck and the mainland. ''You're not staying overnight?'' Bryce persisted. ''Charles will be disappointed.''

''Hardly,'' she snapped, glaring at him.

''I got the impression a couple of minutes ago that he'd like to see more of you. That he feels badly you haven't been on Manatuck for so long...I hope you've sent him an invitation to your show.''

He was being unforgivably intrusive. Not to say rude. Julie was gaping at him, while Travis seemed to be struggling not to laugh. Had Travis really sent his best friend to Wellspring in the hopes that Bryce and Jenessa would fall for each other?

You're right out of luck, buddy. No way am I taking on your kid sister.

Then, like a sledgehammer, a horribly obvious thought hit him between the eyes. He, Bryce Laribee, had taken Travis's sister to bed when she was just seventeen years old.

Travis would kill him if he ever found out. Kill him and ask questions afterward.

''Are you okay, Bryce?'' Julie asked, resting her arm on his sleeve. ''You look as though someone's just hit you on the head.''

Julie was far too acute; Bryce made a manful effort to get himself under control. Smiling into her emerald-green eyes, he said lamely, ''Yeah...sorry. You'd think I'd be used to jet lag by now. But these short trips are always murder on the system.''

''We're going to stay overnight. I think you should, too.''

''I'll see how I feel later on. That's a gorgeous hat, by the way.''

Julie's hat, wide-brimmed and the exact shade of her eyes, was perched on the gleaming dark cap of her hair. ''Travis found it for me,'' she said, giving her husband the smile that always hurt something deep inside Bryce. He was never going to love anyone that much. Because the reverse side of love was the terrifying vulnerability it brought; he couldn't imagine how Travis or Julie would survive if anything happened to the other.

Not for him. No, sir.

As Travis put his arm around his wife's shoulders, pulling her to his body, something else was all too obvious to Bryce: their sexual accord. They made no secret of the fact that they adored each other, in bed and out.

Yet a year ago, Travis had been as much a confirmed bachelor as he, Bryce, was now. Take it as a warning, Bryce told himself. Stay away from Jenessa Strathern. Because if ever anyone spelled trouble, she did.

Maybe it was time he found himself another woman. Pronto.

Then, to his great relief, Travis said, ''Oh, there's the clergyman. I think we should head down that way.''

''Let me wheel the carriage,'' Jenessa offered. She, too, had noticed how tightly strung Bryce was; and she'd been watching surreptitiously while he'd been talking to Leonora and then to Charles and Corinne. Surely he hadn't guessed who she was? She'd made such an effort today to dress in a way that was the antithesis of that funky art student with the purple eyes.

She released the brake on the English pram that had been one of the several gifts her father had showered on his granddaughter, and wheeled it down the slope, aware through every nerve in her body of Bryce walking behind her. The font had been set up on a concrete pedestal; the clergyman in his long robes was waiting for them. She took her position beside her brother, and drew in a slow, calming breath, doing her best to banish thoughts of Bryce. This wasn't about Bryce. It was about her little niece, Samantha; inwardly she vowed to do her best for a child she loved dearly despite her inexperience with babies.

Bryce stationed himself beside Julie, who had picked up her daughter and was holding her in her arms. The baby's long dress was dazzlingly white in the sunshine.

His mother had abandoned him when he was four. Walked out the door and never come back. His father had vanished the same day.

Bryce slammed these thoughts back where they belonged. Buried deep in his psyche. Ignored. Something that had happened so long ago it had no relevance to him as an adult. His financial success had insured he'd never be poor again, or have to go begging for a home. And that was that.

The old, poetic words of the baptismal service fell one by one against his ears. Samantha's parents would always love her, he'd swear to that; the thought of Travis or Julie abandoning Samantha was more than he could conceive. As for him, he'd do his bit to the best of his ability.

When the cool water touched Samantha's forehead, she woke up, gazing around with her big blue eyes. Then she was passed to Jenessa, who repeated her vows in a steady voice that Bryce found almost unbearably touching.

He was the least sentimental of men. What was wrong with him? Was he losing it?

He stole a sideways glance at her and as quickly looked away, feeling as though he'd intruded on a moment that was intensely private. Nothing to do with him.

All too soon, Jenessa was crossing in front of Travis and Julie, walking as gingerly as if Samantha was made of the most fragile crystal. As she held the baby out to him, her face looked soft, gentled in a way he'd never seen it before. He wanted to kiss her so badly he could taste it. Or, at the very least, stroke the smooth curve of her face from her brow to her lips.

Then she smiled at him, a sweet smile that penetrated every one of the barriers he'd lived behind for as long as he could remember: as though the barriers had ceased to exist. "Your turn," she said quietly. "Have you got her?"

On his visits to Travis and Julie since Samantha was born, Bryce had admired the baby, patted her on the head and lavished her with presents; but he'd avoided having to pick her up. Rather cleverly, he'd thought. Certainly neither Travis nor Julie had ever insisted he do so.

But now he was caught.

Jenessa's hand slid from under his, her breast brushing his sleeve as with exquisite care she transferred Samantha from her arms to his; then he was holding Travis's daughter. She felt more substantial than Bryce had expected, wriggling in a way that made him tighten his grip in sudden fear that she'd fall from his hold. Instantly her little face crumpled. To his horror she started to whimper.

He did his best to pay attention to the clergyman, repeating the words he'd carefully rehearsed that morning on the plane. Samantha was bawling now, straining against him, her little face bright red and streaked with tears, her tiny mouth quivering pitiably. He could subdue an entire boardroom and make them listen to him; he could solve complicated problems with a creativity that had helped build his fortune and his reputation. But a ten-pound baby was more than he could handle.

Crossing in front of Julie, Travis came to his rescue. "Here, I'll take her. Shush, Samantha, we're almost done."

As though a switch had been flipped, Samantha stopped crying and smiled angelically at her father. A ripple of laughter ran through the guests. The benediction was pronounced and Bryce heaved a sigh of relief, running his fingers around his collar. Charles, Corinne and Leonora gathered around, cooing at the baby. Momentarily forgetting that he was furious with her, Bryce said to Jenessa, "Thank goodness that's over."

"It's only just begun," she said innocently. "You've promised to comfort and support her all her life."

He raked his fingers through his hair. "The thought makes me tremble. Do you think Charles is going to serve anything stronger than tea at this shindig?"

"If not, I'm sure someone will be able to rustle up some rum to add to your cup."

Her teeth were very white; she looked so carefree and happy when she laughed. When had he ever felt so strongly pulled toward a woman?

Grimly Bryce answered his own question. Twelve years ago, that was when. He'd buried that memory along with so much else. But at the time it had shaken him to the roots to realize that the panting, writhing creature in his arms in that hotel room was a virgin; and it had taken every ounce of his resolve to pull himself off her.

That, of course, was before he'd found out she was seventeen.

Had every woman since then simply been a substitute? Had he ever again experienced such a tumult of desire as had overwhelmed him that night? Maybe it wasn't coincidence that a few months after he'd met Jenessa, he'd made some major changes in his lifestyle.

Hating the direction his thoughts were taking him, Bryce watched her face subtly change. "What's the matter?" she said uneasily.

Before he could answer, Charles had come up to the two of them. "A lovely ceremony," he said gruffly, patting his daughter on the arm. "I'm so glad you were able to attend, Jenessa."

Any vestige of laughter vanished from Jenessa's face. She said stiffly, "I'd do a great deal for Samantha."

"Corinne and I hope you'll be able to stay overnight. It's your first visit to Manatuck in years, you mustn't leave too soon."

"Unfortunately I have to go back this evening," she said with a noticeable lack of regret in her voice. "Artists don't sit around and wait for inspiration to strike—they work for their living."

"Indeed they do," Charles said. "We hope you'll send us an invitation to your opening, I'm anxious to see what you've accomplished."

"I'll speak to the gallery owner," Jenessa said crisply.

"Fine, fine. Now I'll let you talk to your mother."

Charles removed himself in a way that enabled him to smile vaguely in Leonora's direction without actually having to speak to her. Bryce smothered his amusement. This gathering of Stratherns was land-mined with potential disasters. A wife who'd supposedly died, a second wife who hadn't known she existed, a husband who'd lied his way out of the whole mess and estranged himself from two of his three children...maybe his own situation wasn't so bad, Bryce thought cynically, and stayed exactly where he was so he could observe Jenessa and her mother.

While Leonora looked elegant and assured in her silk pantsuit, Bryce could tell that she was very much on edge. "Hello, Jenessa," she said. "I'm pleased to see you, and I'm delighted you're Samantha's godmother. She's a sweetheart, isn't she?"

Little lines of strain were bracketing Jenessa's mouth. But she replied politely, "I'm not sure Bryce would agree."

"I was afraid I'd drop her," he said. "Especially when she started to howl."

Leonora laughed. "She's got excellent lungs. Are you staying for long?"

"Not sure," Bryce said.

"No," said Jenessa.

Leonora looked straight at her daughter. "If I may, I'd like to attend your opening in July."

"It's a long way for you to come," Jenessa said.

"Not really. There's a shuttle between New York and Boston."

"Then I'll see you get an invitation."

"Thank you. Now will you both excuse me? I want to congratulate Corinne on her roses."

Gracefully Leonora walked away, her head held high. Bryce said tightly, "Well done, Jenessa. The fine art of insulting someone without actually being rude—you've got it down pat."

Jenessa looked around. Momentarily she and Bryce were isolated from the other guests, who were drifting down the slope toward the gaily decorated tent where luncheon was waiting. "Perhaps you could learn something from me," she said sweetly, "since your insults go hand in hand with rudeness."

"I haven't known Leonora for long, but I'll tell you one thing—she's a fine woman."

"I never said she wasn't!"

"She's your mother, for Pete's sake. You'd talk to your cleaning lady with more warmth."

"I don't have a cleaning lady—I can't afford one."

"Come off it. Charles is one of the richest men in the state."

"My financial status is nothing to do with you." Jenessa turned on her heel, throwing her words back over her shoulder as she headed for the tent. "This christening is hard enough without you setting yourself up as judge and jury. Leave me alone, Bryce. I'll do my part for Samantha and you can do yours. Just because we're her godparents doesn't mean we have to like each other."

A couple of the guests were glancing her way, curious about her raised voice. Bryce stayed where he was. He could afford to wait. After the luncheon was over, most of the guests would be going back to the mainland. He'd make sure Jenessa wasn't among them, and then he'd have the confrontation with her that was surging through his body like an ocean storm.

It wasn't a fight about money. Or about Leonora, angry though it had made him to hear Jenessa treat her mother so off-handedly. Nor was it about her emotional distance from her father. That, knowing what Travis had told him, he could forgive.

No. It was about a young art student who'd lied to him twelve years ago. About her age and about her identity.

Lies that he, for all his experience with women, had fallen for.

CHAPTER FIVE

LUNCHEON was served in the dappled sunlight of the garden. A chamber orchestra played Mozart and Strauss; white-jacketed waiters looked after the guests with smiling efficiency, plying them with food and the best of wines. The seafood hors d'oeuvres, the salads, chicken in phyllo and raspberry pavlova were all delicious.

On the surface Jenessa carried her share of the conversation with wit and charm, chatting with people she'd never met before and probably never would again. But inwardly she was much too uptight to enjoy herself, restricting her wine to one glass and nibbling at her food. Bryce, so she'd noticed as soon as she'd taken her seat, had positioned himself as far from her as possible. He was giving every appearance of having a wonderful time.

She'd leave right after lunch. She was horribly afraid that if he hadn't already guessed her double identity, he soon would.

She should never have come.

She should never, with all the ineptitude of a teenager, gone to bed with a successful, ruthless entrepreneur who was her brother's best friend. What had she been thinking of?

His body. That's what.

Which was just about all she'd been thinking of today, too. Smothering an inner moan of despair, she did her best to comment intelligently on the Impressionistic paintings at the Boston Museum of Fine Arts. Coffee and tea were now being served in transparent bone china cups decorated with gold. Another hour and she'd be back on the launch.

55

It couldn't be too soon.

But as luncheon wound to a close, Julie came over to her, and in a stage whisper said, "Once the crowd's dispersed, we're all heading for the pool and the hot tub."

"I've got to go home," Jenessa said.

"Oh, no, you can't!" Julie said, looking so disappointed that Jenessa felt instantly guilty. "Not yet. What time's your flight?"

"Well, not until eight-thirty. But—"

"You've got loads of time, then. Do stay for a while, Jenessa. You haven't had the chance to talk to my parents, have you? And you and I get so little time together. As you know, Travis and I are going to Mexico in a couple of months."

Travis acted as a consultant in various tropical countries, while Julie was a physiotherapist who'd worked overseas for years. Jenessa said bluntly, "Bryce Laribee may be my brother's best friend. But I find him rude and abrasive, and I'm not anxious to spend any more time than I have to in his vicinity."

Julie frowned. "He was kind of rude to you, wasn't he? I don't know what that was all about...he's normally charming with women. And most of them are all too ready to be charmed."

"Not this woman."

"You've got to admit he's a hunk."

"Hunkdom can go only so far," Jenessa said loftily.

"You're too pure-minded," Julie teased. "You will stay though, Jenessa?"

The alternative was to sit in the Portland airport reading a paperback about post-structuralism. "Okay," Jenessa said reluctantly.

Julie linked her arm with Jenessa's. "I'll stand guard and make sure Bryce keeps his distance."

The pool was protected from the Atlantic winds by vine-clad, columned lattices and a luxuriously appointed lounging area complete with bar service. Dipping her toe in, Jenessa discovered the water was deliciously warm. Corinne had produced a brand-new bikini for her, and so far Bryce was nowhere in sight. Quickly Jenessa dived in.

She had the pool to herself, as Travis and Julie had disappeared to feed and change Samantha; and she loved to swim. Masefield, the township nearest to Wellspring, boasted a pool, and she swam there at least once a week. She began doing laps in a smooth overarm crawl, feeling her muscles loosen and the tension seep from her spirit. By the time she'd done ten lengths, she decided she'd been exaggerating both her reaction to Bryce and the fear that he might recognize her.

Breathing easily, Jenessa turned at the far end of the pool. She'd leave on the launch at around five-thirty; in the meantime, she could count on Julie to help deflect Bryce's attention. Then, as though she'd called him up, another swimmer surged alongside her, a man whose blond hair was slicked to his skull. She'd have known his body anywhere, she thought in sudden panic. Had she forgotten anything about him?

Bryce began swimming parallel to her, leaving trails of bubbles in the turquoise water. He was keeping pace with her exactly, his muscular legs finning smoothly, his arms stroking with easy strength.

Jenessa speeded up. So did he. She did an economical tumble turn against the wall of the pool, and with true fury realized he'd done the identical maneuver. Again she increased her speed, her one desire to leave him behind. But gradually in the next two lengths of the pool he outpaced her, so that all she could see was the froth of his wake ahead of her.

Jenessa wasn't one to give up easily. She kicked off hard on her next turn, pushing herself to her limit, and to her satisfaction saw the gap between them narrow. However, as she came level with him, he grinned at her through the turbulent water and pulled further ahead.

She was breathing hard, her legs and shoulders aching;

all her hard-won peace had evaporated in an anger that frightened her with its intensity. Snaking sideways, she stroked to the side of the pool and pulled herself up the ladder, her mood not improved when she saw that she and Bryce had had an audience: Charles, Corinne, Leonora and an older couple she assumed were Julie's parents. "Good try!" Charles called out.

Jenessa would have preferred no one to have witnessed that very childish display of one-upmanship. However, she produced a smile and padded toward the diving board, where she neatly executed a jackknife. When she surfaced, she came face-to-face with Bryce. He said, grinning, "Start your tumble turns six inches closer to the wall—that way you can get more propulsion."

She said coldly, "When I want your advice, I'll ask for it."

"Poor loser, Jenessa?"

"Do you always have to win, Bryce?"

He shook his wet hair out of his eyes. "You're a better diver than I am."

"You're too generous."

He said softly, "Don't push your luck—Jan."

Her wet lashes flickered. "You mean Jen. That's what Travis calls me."

"Jan is what I said."

"Then I don't know what you're talking about."

"Don't tell me there have been so many men in the interim that you've forgotten about a certain hotel room in Manhattan twelve years ago?"

In a great splash, Julie landed in the water beside them. "Last one in's a rotten egg," she yelled at Travis and Brent, who were poised on the edge.

Travis heaved a large red ball into the pool and dived in after it. "Water polo," he gasped as he surfaced. "Bryce and I were on the school team."

Water polo was fine with Jenessa; she'd have walked the length of the pool on her hands and knees to get away from Bryce. The rowdy game that followed had elastic rules and, on Jenessa's part at least, involved swallowing rather a lot of water: her mind was anywhere but on what she was doing.

Bryce knew who she was. He'd made the link between Travis's sister and the funky art student who'd ended up in his bed. A corrosive anxiety slowed all her movements, making her clumsy and inept. But tense as she was, she still couldn't ignore the sleek pelt of wet hair on Bryce's chest, the arc of his rib cage or the deep hollows above his collarbones.

He looked as though he hadn't got a care in the world.

Then Charles joined them, gamely doing his best to keep up. He and Travis began tousling for the ball at the deep end of the pool, both of them laughing; like a knife in her chest, Jenessa saw for herself the new rapport between father and son, a rapport Travis had described to her but that clearly she hadn't trusted.

She would like the same, she thought with painful truth, treading water. But she had no idea how to go about getting it. Whenever she contemplated making approaches to her father, the past stepped in between them, large and dark and immovable, like a huge boulder or a heavy piece of Victorian furniture.

Maybe it was all her fault. Maybe the reason she'd never fallen in love had nothing to do with Bryce's repudiation of her, but with a lack in herself. The inability to love. An inner failure that made her unable to connect either with her father or with a potential mate.

Bryce said sharply, "You okay, Jenessa?"

She gaped at him as if she'd never seen him before, her blue eyes pools of pain. He took her by the shoulder. "What's the matter? Have you got a cramp?"

"Yes," she gasped, seizing on the excuse he'd given her, "I'll get out for a few minutes. It's your turn at the far end, you'd better go."

She hauled herself up the ladder, grabbed a monogrammed towel and swiped it over her face and hair. Then she hurried off toward the change rooms. But on the way Corinne beckoned her over, introducing her to Julie's parents, who were positioned on one side of her; Leonora was on the other. Jenessa did her best to hold up her end of the conversation, keeping one eye on the pool; as soon as she decently could, she made her escape.

Quickly she changed into slim-fitting khaki pants, a silk shirt and an embroidered vest, wringing out her wet hair and braiding it to get it out of the way. It was only four o'clock. But there was no reason she couldn't take the launch in the next fifteen minutes, and every reason to do so.

Bryce had guessed who she was. And if she knew anything about him, he was spoiling for a fight.

She didn't have to oblige.

Slipping her feet into her loafers, she left the wet bikini on the plastic stool and opened the door. Bryce, wearing denim shorts and a T-shirt, was standing not ten feet away.

"I've been waiting for you," he said.

"I have to say my goodbyes. Then I'm getting the launch."

"Not before we have a talk," he said, putting an arm around her waist and almost lifting her across the ceramic-floored atrium.

He was fast removing her from the vicinity of the pool. "Put me down," Jenessa hissed. "Who do you think you are, Attila the Hun?"

"I'm a man who wants a few answers," he said curtly, "and plans on getting them. In the next five minutes."

"You know what your problem is? You're too used to getting your own way."

He gave her a wolfish grin. "I like getting my own way. Why wouldn't I?"

He was now propelling her up the gradual slope of the lawn toward the great gray bulk of the castle. "Are you going to lock me in the keep?'' she seethed. ''How very melodramatic.''

''I'd like to keep you locked up,'' he snarled.

''Cute pun—''

''Then I'd make love to you day and night for a whole week and see if that'd fix whatever the hell's wrong with me.''

''Oh, you would, would you? If you think—''

''It's all right, Jenessa, I'm not going to do it. Because, frankly, I don't think it would work.'' Then he bent his head, wrapped one arm hard around her shoulders and kissed her with an impressive combination of rage and passion.

In a distant part of her brain Jenessa knew she should resist. But how could she, when she more than matched both the rage and the passion? With reckless ardor she kissed him back, twisting in his hold so that her body was pressed to his. As his tongue flicked against her teeth, she opened to him, feeling his other arm grasp her hips and pull her even closer. He was fully aroused; faint with longing, a golden haze of desire behind her closed lids, she moved her own hips against his with a sensuality that had lain dormant for a long time.

As suddenly as he'd seized her, Bryce let go. She swayed against his arm, her blue eyes dazed, her lips swollen from his kiss. ''You're right,'' she croaked, ''a week wouldn't be long enough.''

He made an indecipherable sound compounded of frustration and fury, and half dragged her into the shadows of the tall lilac bushes that hugged the stone walls. The lilacs were in full bloom, spires of purple and white sweetly scenting the air. ''Now,'' he said grimly, pulling her around to face him, ''you're going to come clean.''

Twelve years since Jenessa had felt the pangs of desire; yet Bryce, it seemed, could turn them off at will. Fine, she thought. Two can play that game. ''No, I'm not!'' she blazed. ''You're going to listen to me for a change. And we're not going to talk about you and me, we're going to talk about Leonora. I know she's my mother, and I know I'm keeping her at a distance. But there's a reason for that, Bryce Laribee, a very good reason, and before you condemn me out of hand, you're going to hear my side of the story.''

"I'm not—"

"Travis once told me about his earliest memory of Leonora...how she was filling a copper bowl with purple lilacs, ones just like these. He thought her hair was like the black waves on a winter sea, he told me that, too. Don't you see? Travis *had* a mother, he remembers her, he was held by her and she read him stories...but I never knew her. She left when I was a baby, I might just as well never have had a mother. But now everyone seems to expect me to open my arms and call her *mom* and act like a proper daughter. I can't do it! She's a stranger to me, a complete and utter stranger.''

"Everyone we meet starts out as a stranger," Bryce said in a voice as unyielding as the rough-carved stone wall behind him.

"For my entire life I was told she was dead!''

"Yes, your father lied to you, and that was a terrible thing to do. But he's doing his best to make amends, and Leonora desperately wants some kind of relationship with you." The anger died from his face. "Be very careful, Jenessa—don't substitute your art for real life. That's a dead-end street.''

His words struck Jenessa to the core. Dumbfounded, she gazed up at him. Hadn't she been artistically stuck for the better part of a year? Reworking old themes, unable to substitute new ones, yet still driven to cover canvas with paint day after day...she pressed her hands to her ears in an unconsciously theatrical gesture. "I don't know what you're talking about.''

"I think you do." For the first time there was something approaching compassion in his gray eyes. "In fact, I know you do."

That he should know her better than she knew herself infuriated Jenessa. "Bryce, you didn't haul me up here to talk about art."

"I didn't haul you up here just to talk about your mother, either. Why did you lie to me all those years ago?"

"Which lie are you referring to?" she said with conscious provocation.

"Your name. Your age. Your sexual experience. Your relationship to Travis, who happens to be my best friend. Any or all of the above."

"If you'd known I was seventeen, you wouldn't have gone near me. The same goes for my virginity."

"Why did you want me, Jenessa?"

"Julie's thirty-one years old and madly in love with my brother and she thinks you're a hunk. Why wouldn't I, at seventeen and not madly in love with anyone, think the same?" Jenessa gave an offhand shrug. "You're a very attractive man—I'd bet my little Quaker house I'm not the first woman to tell you that."

"Let's skip the flattery," Bryce said in a deadly quiet voice. "You knew about my friendship with Travis, yet you went to my hotel room knowing damn well what was going to happen. What were you doing, settling some kind of score with him?"

"No!" she cried, stung.

"No? How do you think he's going to feel if he ever finds out about that night? That I had his seventeen-year-old sister in bed with me?"

His voice had risen. Jenessa said furiously, "Why don't you just stand on the nearest turret and yell it to the four winds? I was homesick and you were a connection to my older brother, whom I adored. Okay, so I wasn't thinking very straight, I give you that. But you did your best to seduce me. Aren't you in danger of forgetting that?"

"You used me," he said flatly.

Not for anything was she going to divulge that he was the first—and only—man ever to arouse such passion in her. That, too, was her secret, and so it would remain. "You weren't in love with me," she answered coldly. "So you were using me, too."

"And how many men have you used since then? If I was the first, I'm sure I wasn't the last."

"I'm not interested in your sexual history," she lied, "so why should you be in mine?"

"I don't like being deceived. Made a fool of."

"I was seventeen!" she cried. "On my own for the first time in my life, in one of the biggest and most exciting cities in the world. So I made a mistake. So what?"

"We could go to bed right now," he said, his gray eyes like gimlets. "That kiss showed me the chemistry's still there. You don't have to get the launch for another hour, and one advantage of this ill-begotten heap of stone is that we can hide without any trouble at all. What's to stop us, Jenessa?"

She took a step backward, wondering if she'd forever afterward hate the scent of lilac. "You don't make love with someone just because you've got a spare hour."

"I didn't say we'd make love," he replied mockingly. "There are one-syllable Anglosaxon words for what we'd do."

"You hate me, don't you?" she whispered.

"You exaggerate your own importance."

Through a haze of misery, Jenessa heard the sound of voices and laughter. She turned around. The whole family was leaving the pool and wandering toward the castle; Travis hailed her, calling out something she couldn't hear. Light-headed with relief, she said, "I wouldn't go to bed with you if you were the last man in Massachusetts. And I'll do my level best to make sure we never meet again."

Knowing Bryce couldn't very well restrain her in full view of her brother, father and mother, she marched away from him, blinking back tears that she was too proud to shed.

When would she ever learn to listen to her instincts? Hadn't they told her, loud and clear, to stay away from the christening? But she'd allowed herself to be persuaded by a tall man with sun-streaked hair and eyes gray as clouds; and all it had accomplished was to open old wounds.

Open old wounds and inflict new ones. Jenessa wasn't sure which was worse. She did know she'd meant every word she'd said: she was going to stay away from Bryce Laribee. For the rest of her days.

CHAPTER SIX

BRYCE had done enough traveling in the Far East that a Boston afternoon late in June shouldn't have posed a problem. But the humidity was cloying, the sun blazed unrelentingly from a sky that was a merciless blue, and the streets and sidewalks were reflecting the heat so that buildings shimmered like mirages. Exhaust fumes stung his throat.

These were the streets he'd escaped from when he was twelve. Turned his back on. Only in the last year or two had he ventured into them once again.

He had an appointment with the director of a newly built women's shelter. He was fact-finding: another step in the process he'd embarked on a couple of months ago.

Occasionally he found himself wondering if he'd been way off base when he'd decided to build and fund a special school for the kids who roamed these streets. Give them, through education, the chance he'd been given, to leave the streets behind and try for a different life.

There were no guarantees it would work. He knew that.

Wiping the sweat from his forehead, he checked the number on an undistinguished brick building squeezed between a pool hall and a bar; and an hour later, head stuffed with information about possible locations and security precautions, started down the four flights of wooden stairs that led to the street. There were no elevators here. No luxuries at all. But a haven, nevertheless.

He was on the second floor landing when a freshly varnished door swung open. A woman's voice said clearly, "Thanks, Marlene. See you next week, and I'll remember to bring the shampoo."

66

Bryce stopped dead, glued to the tiled floor. He'd have known that voice anywhere. But it couldn't be. Not here.

Then the owner of the voice came through the door, closing it carefully behind her. Her blond curls were confined in a thick braid, her jeans and shirt undistinguished. Bryce croaked, "Jenessa?"

She pivoted. Her jaw dropped. *"Bryce!"*

"What are you doing here?"

"I—I could ask the same of you."

"Are you leaving?"

"Yes," she said, "yes, I am."

"Good. Let's go down together."

Side by side they emerged into the blazing heat. "My car's six blocks over," Bryce said. "I never park it around here, it's asking for trouble. Let me drive you wherever you're going."

"I get the subway a couple of blocks from here, and then the bus—I'm going home, Bryce. But thanks for the offer."

He hated the thought of her walking these streets unprotected, even more of her taking the subway. He said with more honesty that tact, "You look tired out."

"Gee, thanks."

"I'll drive you to the bus station."

Jenessa was tired. Tired, hot and discouraged from listening to the same stories from different women week after week. "Is your car air-conditioned?" she said. "That might persuade me."

"Yep. So come along."

He took her by the elbow, steering her across the street. "Come clean, Jenessa—what were you doing at the shelter?"

"I volunteer there. Once a week."

Her sleeves were rolled up; her bare skin felt wonderful to his touch. Even so, his mind made an instant leap. "That canvas I saw in your studio—now I understand how you painted these streets so vividly."

"I don't tell people I come here. That's why I didn't tell you."

"It's a long way from Wellspring," he said, accepting her tacit apology. "And I don't just mean the bus trip."

"It is, yes."

"Why do you do it?" He could see the reluctance in her face, and added impulsively, "You can trust me to be discreet."

She bit her lip. "The whole time I was growing up, Charles didn't want me. Not as I was. Corinne wasn't ever unkind but wasn't overly warm, either; and my mother was never mentioned, as if she hadn't existed. So now I volunteer at a shelter for homeless women. Who are truly homeless. I know it doesn't make much sense."

He stopped, gazing right into her blue eyes. "It makes a lot of sense," he said gently. "You're doing a fine thing, Jenessa."

"It's not much."

"No one can save the whole world," he said. "But if each of us does our bit, it all helps."

"So what were you doing there?"

He should have anticipated that question. As briefly as he could, he filled her in on his plans for the school. "Kim, the shelter director, has a lot of experience of the neighborhood. So I was picking her brains."

"A special school's a wonderful idea," Jenessa said warmly, adding naively, "You must have a lot of money."

"Enough."

"All of it from computers?"

"Didn't Travis ever tell you the story?" As she shook her head, Bryce said, "The school I went to when I was eleven had a brilliant and eccentric math teacher, and for the first time in my life I saw the point of being in a classroom. He got me a computer, paying for it out of his own pocket—he's the one who arranged for the scholarship to Travis's school, because they had an innovative computer department. By the time I was nineteen I'd come up with some programming concepts when the timing had happened to be right, and in the next five years I made a mint.'' Bryce shrugged. ''Technically, I don't need to work. But I get a kick out of problem-solving, and I like the travel.''

''You want your school to do the same thing for the kids here,'' Jenessa said slowly. ''Offer them a way out.''

''Yeah...the math teacher and I became good friends. He died three years ago.''

''Not in poverty, I'm sure, if you had anything to do with it.''

Bryce looked uncomfortable. ''Don't make me into some kind of saint.''

She chuckled. ''If I am, it probably won't last long.'' Glancing at a boarded window spattered with graffiti, she added, ''You went from rags to riches...is this the area where you grew up?''

He dropped her arm, walking a little faster along the garbage-strewn sidewalk. ''Near here. What time's your bus?''

''In a couple of hours. If you don't like to talk about your childhood, Bryce, you can just say so.''

''All right. I don't.''

From her weekly visits, she'd seen and heard enough to understand why. She said humbly, ''You must think I'm a real wimp, complaining about my upbringing.''

Bryce stopped in the middle of the sidewalk. ''Your mother vanished, your father tried his best to make you into someone you weren't, and Corinne spends more time on her goddamn roses than she does on real human beings—no, I don't think you're a wimp. And I'm sorry I came on to you so hard about Leonora at the christening. I shouldn't have.''

Jenessa said roundly, ''Just when I think I have you figured out, you say something that takes me completely by surprise.''

"It's not your job to figure me out," he said, and strode on.

Panting in the heat, Jenessa followed him. He moved like a hungry tiger, she thought. So what did that make her? A tigress, padding along behind him? Or a rather small animal without many defences who could well turn into prey?

She'd seen a whole new side to Bryce today. A man who cared enough to put money and time on the line for boys and girls he'd never met, who might not even give a damn. Intuitively, she sensed that if his school gave only one or two kids a better life, he'd think it was worthwhile.

She didn't want to start liking Bryce. Bad enough that she still lusted after him with the lack of subtlety of a seventeen-year-old, without adding liking and respect to the mixture.

How could she lust after him when her shirt was sticking to her back and she was so thirsty she could drink out of a puddle?

A few minutes later, minutes in which Jenessa couldn't come up with anything to say, she and Bryce reached his car, a sleek dark blue Jaguar which did indeed have air-conditioning. Once they'd left the area, they were soon cruising streets with leafy trees and unsmashed windows. Bryce said, "I'll buy you dinner. I know a little place a few blocks from here. Then I'll drive you to the station."

"Bryce, I'm a mess—no restaurant would let me in."

"Yes, they will. They know me. Anyway, I'm no ad for the well-dressed man."

The restaurant, at the bottom of a flight of wrought-iron steps, had the most wonderful calamari and Greek salad Jenessa had ever tasted. They were seated in a corner; as she took a sip of a flinty red wine, Bryce said, "I'd fully made up my mind when I left Manatuck never to see you again."

Her lips curved in a smile. "Join the club."

"And here we are. Do you believe in fate?"

She looked at him warily. "Is that a trick question?"

He reached over and took her fingers in his, playing with them until she was weak with a hunger that had nothing to do with calamari. "What are we going to do about this? I want you and you want me and you're no longer a virginal seventeen."

"We're not going to do anything," she said forcefully.

"We're twelve years older than we were then, Jenessa. Older and—on my part—possibly wiser," he added with a crooked grin. "I'm not into marriage. But I promise I'd be faithful to you for the duration of whatever relationship we'd have, and I'd do my best to please you. To make you happy."

For some reason that wasn't clear to her, Jenessa felt like crying. Gazing into the jeweled heart of her wineglass, she sought for words that would match his honesty without revealing more than she was prepared to. "I've met lots of men in the last twelve years," she said carefully. "You don't fit the mold, Bryce. You're forceful and charismatic and so sexy you make me weak at the knees. I don't want to have an affair with you. I'd get in deeper than I'm prepared for, and in the long run you'd only do me harm."

"You're not saying you're in love with me?" he rapped.

"No, of course not! But what happens every time you and I are in the same room doesn't feel casual. You make me lose my bearings. My understanding of who I am." She took a gulp of wine. "That may not make any sense to you. But it's the way I feel. So it's no dice as far as an affair's concerned."

He said flatly, "The way I desire you—it's sure not casual. In a very real way, I resent it."

"I'd noticed," she said dryly.

"You're afraid of me."

"I'm afraid of my own body—of what it does to me when I'm in your vicinity," she said with suppressed violence. "Right now I'd like to drag you behind that palm tree and make love to you on the carpet. That's all very well. But then what?"

He suddenly gave her a smile so full of sheer male energy that she found herself smiling back. "I like you," Bryce said. "I like the way you operate."

"Do you? Do you really? Because I'm saying no, Bryce. And I mean it."

"You're telling me the truth."

She wasn't telling him the whole truth, though. Her lashes dropping to hide her eyes, she tackled her roast lamb and herbed potatoes as though she had nothing else on her mind.

After a short pause Bryce said, "How's your work going?"

So he'd accepted her refusal. Somehow she'd expected him to put up more of a fight. "Pretty well. I finished the final painting for the show three days ago, so today I brought it with me and dropped it off at the gallery."

For a few minutes they talked technicalities, Bryce surprising her by the depth and extent of his knowledge of the contemporary art scene. Then he said, "I called up your gallery, by the way, and sweet-talked an invitation to your show. I hope you don't mind."

Her fork stopped in midair. "What happens if I do?"

"I go anyway."

Her temper rising, she demanded, "Why do you want to go to my show?"

"To see your work. Of course."

"Nothing to do with me," she snapped.

"Well, no. You've turned me down, remember?"

So angry she didn't know where to look, and simultaneously decrying her anger as totally inappropriate, Jenessa said, "Both of us had decided never to see the other again. Why don't we just stick with that?"

"We could try. After the show."

"Oh! You're impossible."

"Everything's possible, Jenessa."

"Not with me, it's not," she announced, her cheeks burning with color.

"I get the message. This restaurant makes fabulous baklava, want some?"

"I want to be on the bus by myself, going home to my own place!"

"Where Charles, Corinne and Leonora won't bother you," he said shrewdly.

"Add your name to the list."

Bryce signaled the waiter, ordering two servings of baklava to go. Then he said very casually, "Are you sure you aren't dismissing me too quickly? Aren't you the slightest bit interested in my money?"

Fighting the urge to tip the entire table and its contents into his lap, Jenessa announced, "Bryce, right now I live pretty close to the bone. But next year, when I turn thirty, I inherit my share of my grandfather's trust fund. No, I'm not interested in your money."

"I'm worth a lot more than your trust fund."

"How much money can one person spend?" she flailed. "I'm too busy painting to be out shopping. And owning stuff for the sake of owning it has never appealed to me."

"Something else we have in common," he said. "I got rid of all kinds of stuff a few years ago. For a while, around the time you and I first met, I owned houses in as many countries as you could name, cars in all the garages, and a private jet so I could commute from one to the other. But then it all palled. Overkill, I guess."

It was his honesty that got to her every time, Jenessa thought painfully. "Why wouldn't you buy houses and cars, with your background? And now you're going to build a school instead." She hesitated. "Who did you live with when you were nine and ten? What were you like?"

"You wouldn't have wanted to know me," Bryce said

dismissively. "We should get moving, the traffic might be heavy. Are you ready?"

He'd closed her out of his past as effectively as if he'd slammed a door in her face. "I wish you wouldn't come to my show," she said with a touch of desperation.

He'd already pushed back his chair. Picking up the bill, he said, "I'll meet you at the front desk."

"You make it very clear that your past is off limits," she said furiously. "Why can't you accept that my future is off limits in the same way?"

"Because I don't want to," he said.

Jenessa shoved back her chair, marched to the washroom, and maintained a stony silence all the way to the bus station. As he drew up outside, she said in a clipped voice, "Thank you for dinner and the drive. Stay away from my gallery, Bryce. Because *never* is just fine with me."

He wrapped his fingers around her wrist. "Never's a long time," he said, and kissed her hard on the mouth.

Her body sprang to life, burning with need. As his elbow brushed her breast, her nipples hardened beneath her thin shirt. It would have been achingly easy to have succumbed, to have leaned into his kiss and his body. With all the strength she possessed, Jenessa tore herself free and tumbled out of the car. "I won't have an affair with you!" she cried.

The sidewalk was crowded. A couple of passersby laughed, a few more stared at her as though she was just one more of the city's eccentrics. She slammed the door of the Jaguar and ran inside; it was only when the bus pulled out of the station that she remembered she'd left her baklava on the floor of Bryce's car.

She loved baklava. But she sure didn't love Bryce.

CHAPTER SEVEN

THE members of Jenessa's family all arrived at the gallery within five minutes of each other, as if it had been pre-arranged.

Jenessa was standing near the back of the room, chatting to two congressmen. Her work was displayed to its best advantage, the gallery was full, the food and wine of excellent quality, and a satisfactory number of sold stickers had already been affixed to the paintings. Furthermore, the new full-length silk skirt and matching tunic she'd purchased just for the occasion suited her very well, its soft rose-pink flattering to her skin. Her hair was in a mass of curls around her face, and she was wearing the opal earrings Travis and Julie had given her for her last birthday.

She should have been happy. Ecstatic.

But she wasn't.

She'd come to the gallery this afternoon for a quick preview of the show. As she'd walked from painting to painting, she'd been struck very forcibly by an underlying similarity in style and theme. Many viewers might not notice, for her talent was real and she was technically very accomplished. But she'd noticed.

Stuck.

It wasn't the first time Jenessa had used this word. But it was the first time she'd been so convinced that it was the right, the only, word.

What could she do about it? How could she push beyond her limits, find what was waiting for her?

She had no idea. Nor was she any closer to an answer as the show opened and the crowd gathered, the energy in the room humming around her. She felt like an actor in a play she didn't believe in. Successful Young Artist Has Brilliant Opening. Except, under the surface, it wasn't brilliant.

Charles walked through the door first, holding it open for Corinne, Julie and Travis. Two minutes later, Leonora entered. After Jenessa had excused herself from the congressmen, she crossed the room to greet her family. At least Bryce hadn't come, she thought thankfully.

"Great crowd," Charles remarked, not quite able to hide his surprise.

"I've been looking forward to this all day," Corinne said with uncharacteristic warmth. "Ah, here's Leonora...good evening."

"Nice to see you, Leonora," Charles said manfully, shaking hands with his first wife.

Julie embraced Jenessa, Travis kissed her cheek, and Leonora said, "How lovely you look, Jenessa."

Leonora looked dauntingly elegant in a gossamer gray outfit that accentuated her poise and slender grace. As Jenessa murmured a commonplace reply, other words dropped into her mind like an ambush. *I'm frightened of my mother,* she thought, and realized it was true.

It wasn't the best of moments for such a realization. She said hastily, "Why don't all of you look around and we'll talk later?" She managed to produce a smile. "I have to circulate. The gallery owner's phrase, not mine."

"Go circulate, Jen," Travis said with his lazy grin. "We're in no rush."

It was on the tip of her tongue to ask if Bryce was coming; but she didn't want Travis to know that it mattered to her. Quickly Jenessa allowed herself to be caught up by those in the crowd who wanted to explain her paintings to her, and those who wanted her to do the same thing for them. She wasn't sure which was worse; but at least it took her mind off her family and Bryce.

Half an hour later, when the noise level was at its highest pitch, a hand fell on Jenessa's shoulder from behind. Her smile froze to her face. How could she know, without even seeing him, that the hand belonged to Bryce?

Because her body was on fire.

Swallowing, she turned around. "Hello, Bryce," she said cordially. "So *never* lasted ten days."

"But who's counting?" he replied with equal cordiality, letting his hand drop to his side. He'd seen a lot of gorgeous women in his life; what was it about Jenessa that had the power to slice him to the core?

With a bit of luck, his reaction to her was well hidden. Because, of course, he had been counting the days until he saw her again. Today, he'd even been counting the hours.

She looked utterly and beguilingly beautiful, her cheeks rose-pink, her eyes that brilliant, combative blue, her silk outfit hinting at the body beneath. No wonder he'd been wishing his life away until he saw her.

He should keep two facts in mind. She didn't want to have an affair with him. And he wasn't willing to offer anything other than an affair.

How could he break that impasse?

By dint of a couple of casual questions, he'd found out that Travis had booked his sister into one of the city's finest hotels. "Didn't want her driving home alone late at night," was what Travis had said.

Neither did Bryce, although for different reasons.

Jenessa said snappishly, "I wish you'd stop staring at me. Have I got lipstick on my teeth?"

He pulled himself together. "No...you look very beautiful," he said truthfully, and watched her blush. "You also look uptight. What's wrong?"

"Charles, Corinne and Leonora are all here," she said glibly. "That's enough to make anyone uptight."

"I was hoping you'd given up deceiving me when you were seventeen. What's really the matter, Jenessa?"

To his horror a film of tears suddenly glimmered in her

eyes. She blinked them back. "Go away, Bryce, I'm the star of the show and I can't afford to be caught blubbering on your shoulder."

"It's available anytime," he said slowly. "We'll go for a drink when this bash is over."

"Best offer I've had all night—which doesn't mean I'll accept it," she said crisply, and gave a mauve-haired, diamond-bedecked matron a dazzling smile. Bryce, frowning, turned away. An affair meant just that: an affair. A careful distance maintained; two separate lives that met in bed to the mutual pleasure of each. And now he was offering Jenessa his shoulder to cry on?

That sort of intimacy was strictly against his rules. Always had been.

He started wandering from canvas to canvas, his height giving him an advantage over the crowd; and as he did so, his frown deepened. In the next half hour he learned a lot about Jenessa. All the paintings were exquisitely rendered, some realistic, others full of mysterious swirls of color that bordered on abstraction. Yet each of them breathed an underlying menace, a threat never explicated enough to be challenged, yet too deeply rooted to be overcome.

That she was, deep down, very unhappy was utterly clear to him. That she was a complex and sensitive artist was also clear. Both these conclusions made him extremely uneasy.

Jenessa Strathern wasn't his usual type. He liked rational, cool women who, if they had hidden depths, had the sense to keep them hidden: in the same way that he guarded his own secrets.

He hadn't been paying attention to anything other than the paintings. To his dismay, Bryce suddenly realized he'd ended up in the middle of a gathering of Stratherns that included the artist. Trying to smooth the frown from his forehead, he greeted them all pleasantly. "A fine show, Jenessa," he said sincerely, "you're to be congratulated."

Charles, who had obviously not understood the paintings at all, said valiantly, "Very pretty colors. Corinne and I bought one that will go with our living room in Back Bay."

"You bought one?" Jenessa repeated, taken aback.

"We're proud of you," Charles said gruffly.

"Oh," said Jenessa.

She looked dumbstruck. Into a silence that was lasting too long, Travis said cheerfully, "Julie and I will have to go soon, sis, because of the baby-sitter. But we'll see you at the hotel for lunch tomorrow. Why don't you join us, Leonora?"

"Unfortunately I'm getting the night flight back to Manhattan...I'm teaching a class first thing tomorrow morning."

"So you came all this way just for one day?" Jenessa blurted.

Leonora smiled. "I did. And glad of it."

Clumsily Jenessa muttered, "Thank you."

"A pleasure," Leonora responded. "Does anyone want to share a cab with me?"

Corinne said smoothly, "What a good idea. Ready, Charles?"

"Of course. Of course, a fine idea." He looked straight at his daughter with his faded blue eyes. "I hope we'll see you again before too long, Jenessa."

Jenessa mumbled something indecipherable, her fingers pleating the silk of her tunic. There was a general exodus, during which Travis drawled, "Coming, Bryce?"

"I want to take another look around now that the crowd's thinned a bit," Bryce said. "I'll talk to you tomorrow."

In the last few minutes he'd been keeping track of all the changes of expression on Jenessa's face, from uncomfortable and disconcerted to trapped. She now looked panic-stricken. Making a mental note to make sure she didn't slip away without him, he said blandly, "Jenessa, the gallery owner's trying to get your attention."

"So she is," Jenessa mumbled and walked away with none of her usual grace.

By the time Bryce had finished a second perusal of the paintings, the gallery doors had been locked and most of the guests had left. With a possessiveness that part of his brain deplored, he walked up behind Jenessa, putting an arm around her waist. "Ready to go?" he asked. "My car's parked just down the street."

She tensed like an over-nervous race horse; then, gauche as the teenager she'd been, she introduced him to the gallery owner. Bryce said something more or less intelligent about the paintings, the owner suggested Jenessa phone her in the morning and left to supervise the caterers. Jenessa said weakly, "I should get a cab."

"You need a good stiff drink. Come along." Keeping his arm snug around her waist, Bryce steered her toward the door.

Outside, the air was hot and humid, the street alive with traffic. Once they reached his car, Bryce said, "There's a nightclub not far from here where they play great jazz. We'll go there."

Jenessa, for once, didn't argue. Easing her feet out of her high-heeled sandals, she sighed, "That's better. Promise me one thing, Bryce—you won't as much as mention the word art."

He laughed. "I-don't-know-anything-about-art-I-only-know-what-I-like…didn't anybody say that to you tonight?"

She laughed as well, wriggling her shoulders against his leather upholstery. "Nobody but you."

Like a prism splitting sunlight, joy swooped through Bryce's chest in all the hues of the rainbow. Jenessa was sitting here. Beside him. In his car. Deep in his heart, he hadn't been at all sure that the evening would end this way. But it had. And now the rest was up to him.

Joy? Did she mean that much to him?

He wanted her in his bed; that was all.

Bryce set out to charm her, deliberately keeping the conversation low key. The nightclub, where he was a member, was understated yet beautifully appointed. The dance floor was dimly lit, the tables positioned for privacy and the service unobtrusive. They were led to a banquette, where Jenessa sank down into the soft seat with another sigh of relief. After she'd asked for a Brandy Alexander, Bryce ordered a beer and some seafood appetizers. As Jenessa tucked into the food with an appetite he found amusing, they began to talk, exploring each other's tastes in books, television and sports; while she had some strong opinions, she was also willing to consider his point of view. He discovered he was enjoying himself enormously, and was pleased to see that the strain had vanished from her face. Half an hour later, he said lightly, "Want to dance?"

Jenessa was halfway through her second drink. "Does that mean I have to put my shoes back on?"

"You can go barefoot as far as I'm concerned."

There was a note in his voice that sent a shiver down her spine. "This doesn't look like the kind of place where you dance barefoot," she said severely.

"I make my own rules," was Bryce's lazy response.

He'd said exactly the same thing twelve years ago. A second shiver followed the first along her backbone. "Just don't step on my toes."

"That would be counterproductive."

"To what?" she demanded.

"To your enjoyment, of course...what else?"

She liked fencing with him, more than liked his rapier wit and the glint of steel in his gray eyes. Throwing caution to the winds, she said, "Let's dance, then."

There were several other couples on the floor. The slow, smoldering melody coursing through her veins, Jenessa slipped into Bryce's embrace. One hand was splayed on her hip; the other clasped her own hand and brought it to his shoulder. Her forehead dropped to his other shoulder, against the hardness of bone and the taut muscle beneath the fine wool of his jacket. As though she didn't have a worry in the world, Jenessa surrendered to the music and the man, allowing herself to drift in a tide of sensuality. Her hunger wasn't hot and imperative this time, as it usually was. It was slower and deeper and—she recognized this—infinitely more dangerous.

She'd played it safe for twelve long years. Was that all she wanted from life? To be safe? Could that be the root of her inability to love?

Wasn't that also what was wrong with her paintings...a fear of taking risks?

She wasn't just an artist: she was a woman. In Bryce's arms she felt her femininity fully and with a pride that was new to her. As he drew her closer, pushing her mass of hair away so that his lips could trace the long line of her throat, she trembled like a leaf in the wind; her tiny whimper of pleasure couldn't have been heard by anyone but him.

Then she raised her head to meet his eyes, making no more attempt to mask her desire than he was to hide the erection that pressed into her body. He said softly, "I want you to know something. There's only one woman I've wanted as much as I want you right now—and she was scarcely a woman all those years ago."

Jenessa smiled, a slow, secret smile. "You mean me?"

"You don't need to ask."

She moved her hips suggestively against his, looking at him through her lashes. "When I said I wanted to sketch you that night, I was telling the truth. But only part of the truth."

"I knew that at the time." He lifted her hand to his lips, kissing her fingertips one by one, then burying his mouth in her palm until she dissolved into nothing but a passionate hunger for more. For greater intimacies she could scarcely imagine. For their two bodies naked together in a bed of his choosing.

She said faintly, "I'm booked into a hotel overlooking the harbor."

"The Colonial?"

She bit her lip. "I've done it again, haven't I? Lied to you. Ten days ago I said I wouldn't have an affair with you. Ever. Yet now I'm telling you I'm staying in a hotel overnight...I'm pursuing you."

Bryce said huskily, "Jenessa, you're honoring me. With the gift of your body."

He meant it, she thought. More than that, he understood that what is valued must be freely given.

For a moment sheer terror gripped her throat. She forced it down, allowing herself to be led back to their table, where she fumbled for her shoes while Bryce paid the bill. Then, her hips swaying gracefully, Jenessa wove between the tables toward the door of the nightclub. Again, the hot air struck her like a blow, the humidity claustrophobic. She got into the Jaguar, folding her hands in her lap.

The drive to the waterfront seemed interminable, Bryce no more inclined to conversation than she. As desire was inexorably replaced by anxiety, Jenessa's nerves tightened to an unbearable pitch. In a very short time, Bryce would know that she hadn't made love with anyone in the years since she'd ended up in his bed. That she was, at age twenty-nine, that anomaly, a virgin. And what would he conclude?

That she was in love with him? Had been, for years?

Neither was true. But would he believe her? She remembered as if it were yesterday how he'd thrown himself off her in that hotel room in Manhattan; and the contempt that had scored his face when he realized how she'd deceived him. She remembered, too, his more recent anger at Castlereigh, his inability to understand how she could have gone to bed with her brother's best friend.

What was she to do? Nothing about her tentative relationship with Bryce felt casual. An affair with him would tear up her life by the roots. She knew it.

Was that what she wanted? To make love with him in the sure knowledge that sooner or later he would discard her? The pain of that betrayal would belittle anything she'd ever felt. Once again, she'd be abandoned.

How would she bear it?

With a jolt of fear Jenessa saw the harbor gleam silver between two buildings. The name of the hotel loomed into her field of vision. They'd arrived. In a few moments Bryce would leave his car with the valet. Then he'd follow her to her room; and it would be too late to change her mind. She said in a voice that didn't sound at all like hers, "Bryce, I can't! I can't do this."

He swerved into the curb, jamming on the brakes. The car behind him blared its horn. He said, any emotion ironed from his words, "What do you mean, Jenessa?"

"I'm not willing to risk an affair with you. I'm too afraid of the consequences."

"I'll protect you against pregnancy, and I already told you I'd be faithful to you and do my best to make you happy."

"Until you meet someone else."

He banged his fist against the steering wheel. "I'm not out looking for anyone else!"

"But you're not into commitment, either."

"I'm not into marriage—I told you that."

"Then I guess I'm not into affairs."

"Don't give me that," he said in an ugly voice. "Travis has shown me pictures of you and articles about you over the years—and you're always dating this man or that. There've been men all along—why do you have to lie to me?"

Tell him you're a virgin. But the words stuck in Jenessa's throat, as if she'd swallowed a stone. She released her seat belt and scrambled out of the car, noting distantly that Bryce was making no move to stop her. "I'm sorry," she gasped, "I shouldn't have led you on. We mustn't see each other again—it's pointless." Then she slammed the door in his face and ran for the hotel.

The doorman smiled at her. Her heels clicked on the lobby's marble floor, the gilded mirrors throwing back images of a distraught, elegantly clad woman who happened to be herself.

There was no sign of Bryce. He hadn't followed her.

Had she expected him to?

The elevator doors slid smoothly shut behind her. Alone, after so many hours, Jenessa let out her breath in a long sigh. Her feet were killing her and she never wanted to wear this outfit again. The minute she got into her room, after bolting the door, she kicked her shoes off, then hauled her tunic over her head and yanked off her skirt, throwing them on the wide bed.

The covers had been turned down. A gold box of chocolates had been placed on the pillow. If she wasn't such a coward, Bryce's head could have been lying on that pillow right now.

In the mirror over the dresser Jenessa saw another image: her slender body in its brief rose-pink bra and panties, the whiteness of her skin, and the tension in her shoulders. An untouched body, unloved and virginal.

Because that's what she'd chosen. For better or for worse.

CHAPTER EIGHT

JENESSA was up very early the next morning. She'd slept atrociously, the empty expanse of the bed mocking her. Last night she'd had an opportunity to undo the damage of twelve years ago, and she'd refused it. She'd turned Bryce down.

He wouldn't be back. He was too proud for that. Why should he beg for her favors, when there must be a dozen women who'd give him what he wanted? Experienced women who knew the score. Unlike herself.

She dressed in a brief patterned skirt with a white halter top, braiding her hair and inserting long, jangly earrings in her lobes. She took some time over her makeup, wanting to look her best; and finally pulled on thin-strapped azure sandals she'd bought in the sales last fall and hadn't yet worn. Then she went downstairs to buy the morning papers. Her show would have been reviewed; the gallery's name alone would ensure that.

Her arms loaded with newsprint, she ordered a coffee and went outside into the leafy courtyard. Choosing the table that was the farthest from all the others, she sat down, took a big gulp of caffeine and reached for the first newspaper, whose art critic she'd met on more than one occasion; she knew he liked her work. She read his column swiftly. His comments were acute, and almost exclusively laudatory. Relaxing a little, she picked up the paper that employed the city's most influential critic.

This was the article that really counted.

The review took up a third of a page. Her mouth dry, Jenessa began to read. The critic started by applauding her technique, which enabled her to infuse a painting with

86

emotions all the more powerful for being understated; but then he moved to the all-important point that the emotions themselves were becoming repetitive. There had been, so he insisted, no noticeable movement since her last, highly impressive show eighteen months ago. It would be a great shame, he continued, if a young artist with the potential of Jenessa Strathern settled for commercial success rather than artistic growth. She wouldn't be the first, nor would she be the last to follow that path. But stagnation would, in the long run, destroy any possibility that she become a painter of true stature.

A breeze wafted through the birch trees, sprinkling the page with sun and shadow. Tears blurring her vision, Jenessa stared at the printed words, as if by sheer force of will she could make them say something else. Why had she ever expected that a critic as acute as this one would overlook what she herself knew to be true?

She didn't know how to change. If she did, she would.

Dimly she heard footsteps approaching her across the flagstone path. Through the same haze of tears she saw Bryce coming toward her. She jammed her dark glasses on her nose, and hastily folded the paper.

He came to a halt in front of her, then plucked the glasses from her face. She said in a choked voice, "Don't do that!"

"I read the reviews. That's one reason I came."

"I don't need you feeling sorry for me."

"Jenessa," Bryce said impatiently, "all he's doing is pointing out that you need a new direction. If he didn't think you were worth it, he wouldn't bother."

"I don't know where to go from here," she cried. "That's the whole problem. I am stagnating, he's right— I have been for months."

Abruptly Bryce picked up the untidy pile of papers. "Come on, we'll go to my place and I'll make you breakfast and you can tell me why you're so stuck."

That he should use a word she'd so often used herself

was the final straw. "So you saw it, too...last night at the gallery when you were looking at the paintings."

"It doesn't take a fancy critic to figure out that you're unhappy and that you're spinning your wheels."

"Do you know how I feel? As though I was standing around in that gallery last night stark naked."

If she'd expected easy sympathy, she was soon disappointed. Bryce said evenly, "That's what real artists do—they bare their souls in the hope that others will grow from the experience. That's a major risk. But if you don't take it, Jenessa, you're dead in the water."

"I'm the one who's stopped growing! And don't you see what else this means?" She struck the papers with the flat of her hand. "Charles will read these. He's never approved of me being an artist—and now I'm proving him right." She gave a bitter laugh. "He'll probably want a refund on the painting he bought."

"Charles bought that painting because he's trying to repair some of the damage he's done, and the only critic he ever pays any attention to is himself." Shoving the papers under one arm, Bryce grabbed her by the elbow. "We're going to my place. Bacon, eggs and more coffee. In that order."

It was oddly comforting to have her mind made up for her. "I like my bacon burnt," she announced.

"I promise it will be."

Bryce, so Jenessa discovered, owned an immaculately restored, bow-fronted mansion on Beacon Hill, complete with red brick, black shutters and white trim. The interior was cool, the pale walls sparsely decorated with an eclectic collection of contemporary art that immediately claimed her attention. While Bryce busied himself in the kitchen, she wandered through the dining room and living room, admiring his taste, but also, subconsciously, searching for family photos or any other trace of his past.

She found nothing. The tantalizing scent of bacon drew her back to the kitchen, which had granite counters, bleached oak cabinets and sunlight streaming through tall windows that were brushed by the branches of cherry trees. An apron wrapped around his waist, Bryce was scrambling eggs in a Teflon pan. He said absently, as though it was the most natural thing in the world that she should be in his kitchen so early in the morning, "Want to put in a couple more slices of toast? We'll eat in the sunroom."

As Jenessa pushed down the handle on the toaster, she found herself trying to picture the other women who'd shared this peaceful domestic scene with him. One thing was certain. She wasn't the first. Nor would she be the last.

Shaking off her thoughts, she carried the toast to the sunroom. Positioned on the south side of the house, its delicate fig trees and tall palms were interspersed with scarlet and coral hibiscus, the bamboo furniture dappled with a dancing pattern of light and shadow. A long couch was flanked by an array of orchids, the sound of a fountain gently plashing over mossy rocks. As Bryce joined her and they sat down to eat, Jenessa said, "The bacon's got just the right degree of crunch."

He grinned. "I'm a pro in the kitchen at burning things."

"Do you do all your own cooking?"

"When I'm here in Boston. I travel enough that the novelty doesn't wear off."

He began talking about some of his experiences in Europe and the Far East; he was a good raconteur. Jenessa said wistfully, "I've never done much traveling."

"Not with Charles?"

"Are you kidding? But I might visit Travis and Julie in Mexico this winter, that would be nice."

"So Charles made no effort to support you once you left home?"

"I ran away. Defied him. He doesn't like people doing

that.'' She hesitated. ''I looked around your living room for family photos—but I couldn't find any.''

''I don't have any. Why are you stagnating in your work, Jenessa?''

She gave him a level look. ''You refuse to talk to me about your background,'' she said. ''I call that stagnating—and I don't think you're about to tell me why.''

''Anyone ever called you stubborn?''

She widened her eyes. ''Stubborn and Strathern go together, hadn't you noticed that?''

Laughing, they simultaneously reached for the jam, Bryce's hand closing over hers on the smooth glass. She stared in silent fascination at his fingers, so strong and lean, so warm on hers. Then she looked up.

Of one accord, she and Bryce surged to their feet, almost knocking over the jar of jam in their haste. Then she was locked in his arms, the heat of his long body searing her with another heat. Yes, she thought, yes. This time I won't run away.

She pulled his head down impatiently, kissing him with more enthusiasm than technique. He parted her lips with his tongue, and tugged her top free from her waistband, his hands seeking the smooth planes of her back. Then she felt him undo the clasp on her bra; she leaned back, her face open to him as he found the swell of her breast. Her nipple tightened. Her whole body was filled with the sweet ache of desire.

He said roughly, ''When you look at me like that...make love to me, Jenessa. I swear I'll be as good to you as I know how.''

''Yes,'' she whispered. ''I want you so much.''

She reached for his shirt, undoing the buttons one by one, tangling her fingers in the rough blond hair on his chest, then dropping her cheek to lay it against the rapid thud of his heart. Gentle even in his haste, he pulled at the ribbon on her braid. Then he loosened her mass of curls until it tumbled free, surrounding her face. ''The sunlight's caught in your hair," he said huskily. "Like fire."

Scarcely knowing what she was saying, she begged, "Make love to me, Bryce."

He swung her into his arms, lifting her and striding over to the couch. In a tangle of limbs, they lay back, kissing each other with fierce intimacy until Jenessa's heart was thrumming in her breast. He dropped his head, taking one nipple, then the other in his mouth, teasing them with his tongue until she was sobbing with pleasure. His knee was between her thighs; she writhed beneath him, wanting more, always more, until there would be no more to want.

His bare shoulders, the taut arch of his ribs and crest of his hip, step by imperative step she was relearning the geography of the one man in her life who had the power to make her truly herself. Then Bryce fumbled in the pocket of his trousers, extracting a small envelope and dropping it on the floor by the couch. Protection, she thought; she'd forgotten all about it. "You carry that everywhere?" she said blankly.

"The reviews were one reason I went to get you this morning. Making love to you was the other."

"You're very sure of yourself. After last night I thought I'd never see you again."

"I don't give up that easily. Take off the rest of your clothes...I want to see you naked."

And didn't she want the same thing? As he tugged at the zipper on his trousers, with awkward haste Jenessa kicked off her sandals and tossed her lace underwear aside. No barriers, she thought. Nothing between him and me.

Bryce slid between her legs, hard and deliciously silky, all the while laving her breasts with his tongue. She arched toward him like a wild creature, clasping him by the hips. Then his fingers found the wet, enclosing petals between her thighs, stroking her until she cried out his name, again and again, tumbling into wave after wave of pleasure.

He kissed her parted lips, nibbling at their swollen warmth; then, quickly, he dealt with the contents of the little foil envelope. Kissing her again, he muttered, "Jenessa, Jenessa...I can't wait any longer."

She lifted her hips, knowing she was more than ready for him. "I should tell—"

He quieted her with his mouth, plundering it for all its sweetness. Then she felt his first thrust meet her body's resistance. "Bryce, I—"

"Relax, sweetheart..."

That he should use such an endearment melted every bone in her body. Passionately wanting him deep within her, completing her as she'd never been complete, she clung to him, her eyes closed, her inner rhythms seizing her once again in all their primitive strength and beauty. And if there was one feeling that was predominant, it was a deep gratitude that she'd waited for Bryce. Waited twelve long years.

But as he thrust again, she couldn't hide her involuntary gasp of pain. "Don't stop, Bryce," she cried, "please don't stop."

But she was too late. His body had frozen in her embrace, his breathing harsh in her ears. Then he looked up, his gray eyes stunned. "You're still a virgin," he said hoarsely.

"Yes. It doesn't matter, I want you to—"

"But how can you be? All those men..."

She dug her fingers into his shoulders, any vestige of pride long gone. "I don't want to be a virgin any longer, I've waited for you since I was seventeen. I was just dating those men, that's all. But not one of them swept me off my feet the way you did so long ago. The way you do any time I'm near you."

"You're in love with me," he said inimically.

"I'm not! I just refused to settle for less, that's all."

He grabbed her wrists, detaching her fingers with cold precision. Then he pulled himself off her. "Twelve years, Jenessa? Twelve *years?*"

It was happening again, she thought frantically. The same repudiation, the same humiliation: as though there was something shameful about her body's innocence. She reached for her top, trying to cover her breasts, and took refuge in anger. "You'd rather I'd slept with a different man every night of that twelve years? Is that it?"

"I'd rather you'd told me the truth."

"Oh, gee, Bryce, how nice to see you again and by the way I'm still a virgin?"

His eyes were hard as granite. "You've been carrying a torch for me all that time."

"If that were true—which it's not—would it be so terrible?"

"I don't want anyone falling in love with me."

"The way you're behaving, I'm not likely to," she stormed. "What's with you anyway? Are you afraid to admit you've got feelings?"

"Lay off, Jenessa."

"Oh, so you can say whatever you want but I'm supposed to keep my mouth shut? What kind of double standard is that?" She pulled her halter top over her head with trembling fingers. "I went out on a limb this morning. With you. But do you understand that? No way—you're too caught up in your tight little agenda. Too busy protecting yourself."

"Dammit, I'm not!"

"Don't you understand the risk I took? No commitment, you say, and heaven forbid you should get married. So that means that sooner or later in this affair you keep talking about, you'll leave me. Just like my mother did. And my father, too, because he never wanted me. Do you have any idea what it's like to be abandoned by both parents?"

A shudder ran through Bryce's big body. In one swift

movement he stood up, hauling on his trousers. She said in a low voice, "Bryce, I'm sorry...I hit home there, didn't I?"

"You artists are all the same—too much imagination," he said nastily.

"I didn't imagine that reaction! And how else would you end up on the street if your parents hadn't abandoned you?" She too stood up, her top still rucked out of her waistband, her skirt falling to cover her thighs. "Won't you tell me about it?" she pleaded, resting a hand on his arm. "Was it so terrible that you can't share it?"

He said icily, "At least you've got parents. A mother, a father and a stepmother. Imperfect people, all of them. But real. And wanting to connect with you."

"Don't you know where yours are?"

He ignored her interruption as if it hadn't happened. "But you're too bloody stiff-necked to let Charles or Leonora into your life, aren't you? No wonder you're stuck artistically. No sex life, no parents, buried in the countryside like a hermit."

The cruelty of his assessment made her heart go cold within her. She backed away from him, awkwardly stooping to find her underwear and her sandals, pulling them on with no attempt at dignity, then thrusting her halter top back into her waistband. "It's not that easy," she said raggedly. "How can I suddenly love a mother I never knew? One who left me when I was a baby?"

"How would I know? But you're not even trying."

Her dark glasses, the newspapers and her little blue purse were lying on the table. Jenessa picked them all up. "Have you ever searched for your parents?" she said steadily, and saw her answer in his face. "Then don't condemn me for something you're not willing to do yourself...I'll see myself out."

She hurried through the beautifully appointed rooms, blind to anything but her need to find the front door and escape. Struggling with the complicated latch, she let herself out onto the front steps, which were flanked with pots of boxwood. Later on this morning she was having lunch with Travis and Julie; so she couldn't go back to her hotel and cry her eyes out.

Somehow she had to calm down. Look normal.

She had no idea how.

Quickly she walked away along the narrow sidewalk.

CHAPTER NINE

Two days later, a courier delivered a package to Jenessa in Wellspring. She signed for it and went back inside, staring at the package as though it contained a live tarantula. The return address on the top corner was Bryce's, the handwriting forceful and masculine. Like the man himself, she thought. She hadn't left anything behind at his house, she knew that. So what could he possibly be sending her?

One way to find out, Jenessa. Open it.

She poured herself a glass of juice, gingerly picked up the package, and went outside to sit under the apple tree. Ripping off the paper and the bubble wrap, she found a video inside, along with a plain piece of folded paper. Opening it up, she found more of the same terse handwriting. *I borrowed this from Travis,* he'd written. *Sit down and watch it, Jenessa.* The note was signed, simply, *Bryce.*

There was no label on the video to indicate its contents. Intensely curious, Jenessa went inside, turned on the TV and inserted the black plastic cartridge. Within moments she was lost to her surroundings.

It was a video of Leonora dancing. A much younger Leonora, strikingly beautiful, strong, flexible and graceful. The music was totally unfamiliar to Jenessa, atonal, its rhythms not always easy to follow; from this unpromising material Leonora had woven patterns of intricate beauty. Some of the video consisted of retakes, in which the same music would play again, and again Leonora would bend to its demands. Improvising, perfecting, struggling to wrest from the notes a truth that would satisfy her.

The unknown editor of the video had chosen not to omit the cost of these performances to the dancer. Leonora's physical exhaustion, her discouragement and her stubborn determination were all there to be seen.

The final performance was in front of a live audience in Paris ten years ago. As soon as it was finished, Jenessa rewound the tape and watched it again from beginning to end, her eyes intent on the screen. The second time she picked up more detail, the third more again. As the applause died down at the end of the tape after her third watching, she suddenly found herself weeping as though her heart was broken.

This woman was her mother. In her own blood flowed that same struggle to wrest some sort of truth from the intractable stuff of daily life. She understood in her bones Leonora's discouragement, knew the cost of striving for a perfection that could never be attained.

Her mother might have abandoned her as a baby. But in a very real way Leonora had always lived within her.

But hadn't she herself, lately, been guilty of giving up? Of dancing to the same pattern over and over again, unable—or unwilling—to break free?

Jenessa swiped the tears from her cheeks, and for a long time sat gazing at the empty screen. Then she made a phone call to Travis.

That evening Jenessa sat down at the kitchen table, the telephone in front of her. She knew in her heart the step she was about to take was a huge one; knew also there was a very real risk she could be rejected. Taking a steadying breath, she picked up the receiver and punched in the numbers.

"Leonora Connolly," a voice said briskly at the other end.

"This is Jenessa."

After a fractional pause Leonora said sharply, "Is something wrong? With you? Or Travis?"

"No. No, we're fine. I—I just wanted to talk to you."

Leonora's voice warmed. "In that case, I'm delighted to hear from you."

"I wondered if we could get together sometime soon," Jenessa said in a rush. "I could take the Amtrak to New York. If you were willing."

"As it happens, I'll be in Boston at the end of the week, supervising a choreography workshop. Could you come into the city? How about a late lunch on Friday? I'm getting the train back that afternoon."

"That would be great."

Quickly they made the arrangements where to meet. Then Leonora said, "I have to go, Jenessa, I have an appointment in a few minutes. But I'm looking forward to seeing you."

"Me, too," Jenessa gulped, tears gathering in her eyes. To the strength of character that Leonora's video depicted, she now had to add generosity of spirit, and the refusal to hold a grudge.

She put down the phone. She'd done it. Made the first move to heal wounds that had been dealt nearly thirty years ago.

Face-to-face, would Leonora reciprocate?

Filled with nervous energy, Jenessa went outside into the long twilight and dead-headed her roses; in the next couple of days she volunteered at the women's shelter, went swimming, froze beans and peas and made strawberry jam. Carefully, the day she left for Boston, she packed a jar of jam into a basket, along with some freshly picked peas and cilantro.

Dressed in a cool white linen dress, her hair loose, her basket over her arm, she walked to the bus stop in the village. The journey into Boston seemed all too short; her heart thumping in her chest, Jenessa reached their rendezvous on the fringe of the theater district ten minutes early. She walked into the attractive Italian restaurant, found Leonora had made a reservation, and was shown to a table for two in a secluded corner. She sat down, her palms damp, her heart thumping unpleasantly, and buried her face in the menu.

She wasn't the slightest bit hungry.

"Hello, Jenessa...no, don't get up."

Without fuss, Leonora seated herself across from her daughter. Her trouser suit was boldly patterned in black and white; as always, she looked cool and self-contained. They made small talk for a few minutes, before giving their orders to the waiter. Once he'd walked away, Jenessa blurted, "I saw a video of you dancing. That's why I'm here."

Leonora fastened her deep blue eyes on Jenessa's face. "Travis gave it to you?"

"No." Jenessa blushed scarlet. "Bryce did."

"Bryce?"

"After we'd had a fight. One of several. That's when he mailed me the video."

"If it's brought about this meeting, then I owe him a debt of thanks."

"He's the most arrogant, obstinate man I've ever met!"

"Also extremely attractive. I'm not so old that I can't see that," Leonora said, amused.

Hastily Jenessa tried to get back on track. "I didn't come here to talk about Bryce."

Their salads arrived, crisp and inviting. "Jenessa," Leonora said forthrightly, "we can talk about anything under the sun. I'm just so glad to be sitting here with you—I want you to know that."

Again Jenessa's eyes swam with tears. "Thank you," she mumbled. "The trouble is, I don't know where to begin. You see, I'm stuck, I'm stagnating—you can't fix that, I'm not asking you to. But—"

"I read one of the reviews of your show. I thought at the time that stagnating was a very harsh word."

"But it's true. I am. I've known it for some time, but I can't get a handle on how to deal with it. I don't know what to do!'' In a rush of words Jenessa went on, ''Your video—we're so much alike.''

''We are, aren't we? To have our type of temperament is both a blessing and a curse.''

Jenessa gazed at the elegant woman across the table from her. ''I don't even know what to call you,'' she muttered. ''I can't say *mother*. It just doesn't sound right.''

''How about Leonora? It's my name, after all.''

With a watery grin Jenessa said, ''So it is. Okay, I'll do that. Leonora, I've watched your video half a dozen times. You're struggling with truth, trying to discover and express it. That's the essence, isn't it? But there's a truth I haven't found yet, and I don't know the way. So I'm lost. To use Bryce's phrase, I'm spinning my wheels.''

''There was a space of nearly seven months before that video was shot that I couldn't dance, Jenessa. Didn't have anything to say. And that's not the first time that's happened. I do believe that any artist worth her salt goes through fallow periods.''

Jenessa asked an eager question, which Leonora, searching for the most accurate words, answered more than fully. An hour later, her head whirling, Jenessa said in a dazed voice, ''Do you know what? I finally get it— all this time I've been painting Charles. My father. Obsessively. Again and again.''

''That sense of menace that's in all your work?''

''Precisely. From the time I was old enough to notice his reactions, I knew I wasn't the way I was supposed to be. He wanted me to be different. Tried to force me to fit his mold.'' She gave a rueful smile. ''I called Bryce stubborn. I can be just as stubborn, so I resisted Charles with all my might. But he posed a tremendous threat to the way I wanted to live my life. And all these months that's what I've been painting.''

''You understand that in trying to shape you into someone else, he was exorcising me?''

"The woman who ran away from him."

"And was duly punished for doing so."

"But you've forgiven him, haven't you?" Jenessa said slowly.

"Yes, I have...although it took a long time. I'm only sorry that he took out his anger on you and that I wasn't there to protect you. I did run away, Jenessa. But when I flew to Paris I had every intention of returning often to see my children. It was Charles who made sure that didn't happen. Out of anger and pride as much as love."

In a low voice Jenessa said, "I haven't forgiven him."

"You will when you're ready. If I can, I'm sure you can. Because you're right, you and I are very much alike. I dance. You paint. But otherwise we're carbon copies."

Jenessa grinned. "I'm blond, don't forget."

Leonora ran her hand over her dark hair. "Whereas I'm going gray," she said ironically. "One more thing—you and I have a vibrant inner world. But Charles lives by externals. Appearances. By whatever-will-the-neighbors-think."

Jenessa gave a sudden giggle. "Externals? Like Castlereigh?"

"Turrets, moats and battlements..."

The two women dissolved in a gale of laughter. *This is my mother,* Jenessa thought suddenly. *My mother, and we're sitting in a restaurant laughing together.* She said raggedly, "Leonora, thanks so much for agreeing to meet me today. I've been distant and unfriendly ever since you appeared on the scene, and I'm truly sorry."

"You had every reason to be distant."

"I'd like to see you again."

"Why don't we make a date for you to come to New York?" Leonora smiled. "If you get tired of me, there are lots of art galleries."

"I can't imagine being tired of you," Jenessa said honestly, and took out her diary.

After they'd picked out a time, Leonora said, "There

are a couple of things I want to add. Charles is happy that he and Travis are reconciled. I do believe, in his muddle-headed way, your father's doing his best to reach out to you.''

Jenessa's smile was twisted. ''Buying a painting that goes with the decor.''

''It's a gesture that means more than it seems.''

''I'll keep that in mind,'' Jenessa said dryly. ''What was the other thing?''

''It's about Bryce. Travis has told me how he met Bryce, at the private school Travis had been attending since he was six. Bryce and he were both twelve when Bryce was admitted as a scholarship student. Straight off the street. Angry, rough-spoken, untrusting. I don't think even Travis knows the full story of Bryce's upbringing. Probably nobody does but Bryce. You might want to keep that in mind when you're having one of your fights with him.''

''I'm not the least bit in love with him,'' Jenessa said mutinously.

''That's probably just as well,'' Leonora remarked. ''Jenessa, my train leaves shortly, I'm afraid I have to go.''

They both stood up, Jenessa passing over the gifts from her garden, her throat tightening at Leonora's obvious pleasure. Quickly, before she could change her mind, she hugged her mother, and as quickly stepped back. She couldn't cry again. Not here. ''I'll see you next week,'' she said.

''I'll look forward to it.'' Her smile lighting up her face, Leonora gathered her gifts and wove her way between the tables. Jenessa went to the washroom, then wandered outdoors into the heat. Each individual leaf on the trees seemed to be outlined in light; the colored awnings and the yellow cabs were incredibly vivid. I'm happy, she thought. Happier than I've been in a long time. I'm so lucky to have a mother like Leonora.

A smile curving her mouth, she did a little window-shopping, then took a tram to the bus station. She'd decided that morning when she'd left home that she wasn't going to get in touch with Bryce just because she was in Boston. Now, even though she had twenty minutes to wait before she could board the bus, she was determined not to change her mind.

He might be in New Zealand for all she knew. He might be out with another woman.

She sat down on a bench and did a rapid sketch of the beams of light crisscrossing the passersby, her pencil flying over the paper. Then, from memory, she drew Leonora walking toward her in the restaurant.

Leonora, her mother, who understood her in a way Charles never had.

At noon the next day, Bryce was in his bedroom on Beacon Hill, tossing some clothes into his case for a trip to Tokyo and Osaka. His mind was only half on what he was doing. The other half was thinking about Jenessa.

He had to stop this. She obsessed him, night and day. It was crazy. Irrational. And, of course, utterly useless.

All he wanted was an affair. But an affair to Jenessa spelled abandonment.

He knew about abandonment. So how could he push her into a temporary relationship that in the end might hurt her more than it benefited her? He was an expert on balancing cost and reward: he was a businessman, after all.

He had to forget about her. Find himself another woman, if that's what it took.

In an effort to do just that, he'd dated Isabel last night. Isabel was bright, attractive and witty. He'd spent the entire evening wondering what Jenessa was doing. Where she was, and with whom. Tormenting himself by imagining her with another man.

It had to stop. Now.

His phone rang. Scowling, he reached over to the bedside table and picked it up. "Bryce Laribee," he said curtly.

"Bryce, this is Jenessa."

His heart plunged in his chest. He dropped the socks he was holding onto the bed and said tritely, "What a nice surprise."

"Bryce, I—do you have a minute?"

He sat down on top of the socks. For you, all day and all night, he thought, and said briskly, "I'm packing to go to Japan. But I've got a few minutes."

"Oh. I wanted to thank you for sending me the video."

"Have you watched it?"

"I may have worn it out," she said wryly. "I—the reason I'm calling you is because the video made me get in touch with Leonora. I saw her yesterday. In Boston. She was there for a workshop. We talked for two hours, Bryce, it was wonderful. So I'm phoning to say how grateful I am."

She wasn't phoning to say she wanted to jump into bed with him. "Are you still in Boston?" he said sharply.

"No. I'm home."

So she hadn't gotten in touch while she was in the city. He subdued a disappointment as strong as it was illogical—after all, he'd been out with Isabel, what good would it have done if Jenessa had phoned him? "Will you see Leonora again?" he asked, realizing to his inner fury that he sounded as polite as an elderly uncle.

"Yes. I'm going to New York next week to stay for a couple of days...so thank you again for your part in bringing us together. And now I mustn't keep you, you're busy."

Now she was the one who sounded crushingly polite. Exasperated with himself, Bryce said, "Jenessa, I've blown this whole conversation. I really want to see you. Why don't you come into the city next Saturday? We could go to the shore, go for a swim. Have dinner by the ocean.''

In a hostile voice she said, ''I'm still a virgin. That hasn't changed. And I'm not in love with you. That hasn't changed, either.''

''If I booked a chalet on Cape Anne,'' he said hoarsely, ''would you stay there with me? A one-bedroom chalet?'' Had he gone too far?

''Oh, Bryce,'' she said helplessly, ''I don't know.''

Her reply wasn't the one he wanted. He said evenly, ''I'm really glad you got in touch with Leonora, and that you phoned me to thank me. Given that we seem to do nothing but argue.''

''We don't argue, we interface—isn't that the buzz-word?''

''I don't think any of the current buzzwords can cover what happens to me every time I see you. Dammit, Jenessa, I can't get you out of my mind. As for the rest of me, we'd better not go there.''

She said uncertainly, ''So we'd spend the weekend to-gether?''

''Another risk.''

''For me, yes,'' she said with some of her normal spirit. ''But what about you?''

Tell her the truth, Bryce. ''I've never felt this torn, this obsessed. So out of control when it comes to a woman. I don't know what the hell it means. For me or for you.'' He raked his fingers through his hair. ''It's a risk for me too, Jenessa.''

''All right,'' she said in a small voice.

''You'll do it?''

''Yes.''

He found he was grinning, a wide grin that seemed to split his face in two. He said exuberantly, ''You just made me feel like a million dollars.''

''I hope you feel that way at the end of the weekend.''

"No second thoughts. I'll pick you up in Wellspring on Saturday morning at nine."

"That early?"

"If we've only got the weekend, I don't want to waste any of it."

"You've got my phone number if you change your mind," she said darkly.

"I won't. Neither will you. 'Bye for now."

Bryce didn't feel quite as confident as he'd sounded. He reached for the phone book. Pulling strings without any compunction, he booked the most luxurious chalet in the resort. Then he threw his socks into his case.

He'd much rather be going to Cape Anne with Jenessa than to Tokyo on his own. But he'd be back on Friday. He had a meeting late that afternoon with an architect who'd roughed up plans for the school Bryce wanted to build. But then he'd have the whole weekend with Jenessa. Beautiful, argumentative, virginal Jenessa.

He should add another adjective, he thought, snapping the lock on his laptop. Courageous. She'd phoned a mother she'd never known, forging, however tentatively, a new relationship. That had taken guts. It sure wasn't the action of a woman who was interested in staying stuck.

So where did that leave him? He'd never, not once, made any attempt to trace his mother or his father.

He knew why. He couldn't bear as an adult to arouse memories of the violence that had terrorized him as a little boy. The shouting, the blows, the drunken rages...they were all there, deeply buried in his brain.

Waiting for him.

Worse than the violence, though, had been a lasting sense of betrayal. He'd loved his mother, and had taken for granted, as a child does, that she loved him back. But then she'd left him as cold-bloodedly as if he'd been an old shirt she'd tossed to the floor.

He'd buried the pain of that betrayal, too. But wasn't

it one more reason why commitment was, for him, a dirty word?

If he'd never told Travis any of this, how could he tell Jenessa?

CHAPTER TEN

ON SATURDAY morning, when Bryce pulled up outside Jenessa's little Quaker house, it was raining. Not a downpour, but a gentle, steady rain that showed no signs of lifting. He didn't really care. If they spent the whole weekend in bed, that would be fine with him.

How would she feel about this agenda?

He got out of the car and ran for the front door, which was open. Knocking on the screen, he called, "Jenessa?"

"Come on in."

An overnight bag was sitting on the floor by the door. Then she came out of her bedroom, giving him a distracted smile. "Lousy weather for heading to the beach."

"It should clear tomorrow," he said, drinking in her appearance. Slim white pants, a formfitting blue sweater with a scooped neck, and an unbuttoned silk shirt.

She wasn't meeting his eyes. He walked up to her, put his arms around her and kissed her firmly on the mouth. Holding herself rigidly in his embrace, she muttered against his lips, "One minute I want to tear the clothes off your body, the next minute I want to run straight for the Berkshire Hills."

Tilting her chin so she had no choice but to look at him, Bryce said with all the willpower he possessed, "Running away and being stuck are two sides of the same coin."

She blinked. "I suppose you're right."

"Some day soon we'll go to the Berkshires together. I know a wonderful inn beside a river—their chocolate rum pie is to die for. And no, I haven't stayed there with a woman."

108

She said in a strangled voice, "When you decide you want to end this affair, I want lots of warning."

"Jenessa, we haven't even begun! I swear I won't dump you like a bag of garbage, what kind of a guy do you think I am?"

Picking at one of the buttons on his shirt, she said, "I don't know you at all. Not really."

"That's why we're going away together, to find out about each other," he said more gently. "Is this bag all you're taking?"

"And my paint box. I don't go anywhere without that."

"Let's go, then. I've got a thermos of coffee and a couple of Danish in the car."

"When all else fails, eat carbohydrates?"

He laughed. "Are raspberry Danish the way to your heart? You see, I'm learning already."

"If they're Wilma Lawson's, they are." With sudden intensity Jenessa added, "Do you want to learn about me?"

"Yes," he said slowly, "I do," and knew the words for the truth. A truth whose implications were beyond him.

She reached up, kissed him swiftly on the cheek, and backed away before he could respond. "That's a good start. Let's go, I want to smell the ocean."

Wondering if he'd ever understand her, Bryce picked up her bag. Four hours later, he was parking the Jaguar beside a cedar chalet hedged in with evergreens to which the rain clung in bright droplets; the place reminded him of the cottage he owned in Maine. The surf was low, its lazy, murmurous rhythm falling softly on his ears. A gull wailed overhead.

Nothing could be further from the tenement he'd lived in with his parents. But why was he thinking of that now?

He got out of the car, stretched his legs and unlocked the trunk to get their bags. He knew exactly what he was going to do. And how he was going to do it. He said casually, "Want to bring your painting gear?"

Jenessa had been rather quiet ever since they'd stopped for lunch. Bryce walked inside the chalet, glancing appreciatively at the stone fireplace, the polished wood floors and comfortable couch beside tall windows that overlooked the ocean. Quickly he closed the vertical blinds. Then he walked over to Jenessa, picked her up, dropped her unceremoniously on the wide bed and fell on top of her. "Gotcha," he said, laughing.

"I—"

"There's a time for talk, Jenessa, and this ain't it," he said. "Kiss me."

"You're being very dictatorial."

"Twelve years is too long to wait."

"So we're going to make love?" she said, her eyes huge in her face. "Finally?"

"That's the plan. Why don't you close your eyes and kiss me as though right here in bed is just where you want to be?"

She gave a breathless laugh. "But it is. Oh, Bryce, it is."

The softness of her breasts against his chest was driving him out of his mind. Her perfume was subtle, her lips utterly enticing. He felt his groin harden and shifted position, wanting her to take the first step. Willingly and unafraid.

She looped her arms around his neck. "This time you'll let it all happen?"

"All the way."

"Oh, yes…" She drew his head down very slowly, flicking at his lips with her tongue until he thought anticipation would burst his chest open. Only then did she bring him closer, nibbling at his mouth with a sensuality that set his heart pounding. By the time she did kiss him, a deep, passionate kiss, Bryce's head was swimming. He let his tongue dance with hers, lifting some of his weight from her as she moved her hips beneath him in slow circles. He said roughly, ''You're driving me crazy.''

''We've got too many clothes on,'' she whispered.

Raising himself on one elbow, he eased her shirt free of her shoulders, then pulled her sweater over her tumbled hair. Her bra followed. His gaze lingering on the sweet curves of her breasts, he reached for her trousers, pulling them down her thighs. Last of all, he removed her silky underwear. She lay still, her cheeks flushed, as he let his eyes wander over her from head to foot. Then she said faintly, ''You're the only man in my whole life who's seen me like this.''

''I feel as though you're the first and only woman I've ever been with,'' he said, shucking off his shirt and reaching for the zipper on his trousers. As he kicked off his briefs, she was already stroking his chest, playing with his nipples in their tangle of hair, her own hair falling tangled and sweetly scented to his shoulder. Briefly he closed his eyes, wanting to savor every sensation.

She brought her mouth to his chest, slid it downward to his navel, then lower still until she found the hardness that was all his passionate need of her. His stifled gasp of pleasure sounded very loud. Arching over her, Bryce buried his fingers in her hair, allowing her the freedom of his body. The ivory slopes of her shoulders and the long curve of her spine entranced him; how would he ever get enough of her?

When he knew he couldn't bear her caresses any longer, he lifted her bodily, kissing her until he couldn't breathe. Her breasts, the gentle concavity of her belly, the warm, wet folds between her thighs, he found them all, one by one; wishing only to give her what she'd given him, he explored with fingers and mouth and tongue, reining in his own passion to feed hers. His reward was to watch the flames ignite in her irises, and hear her quick, panting breaths, her frantic pleas for more.

Only when he was sure she was ready did he reach for

the foil envelope he'd had the presence of mind to place by the bed. Then he moved to enter her, again forcing himself to hold back, to be as gentle as he knew how. But he had to hurt her. There was no other way.

He saw pain tighten her features, and pulled away. But Jenessa thrust toward him. In a broken voice she cried, "Now, Bryce...now."

Her cry pierced him to the heart; but then she enveloped him in the wet darkness of her body. For a few precious seconds it was as though everything stopped. Her eyes were fastened to his, and in them he saw wonderment and pride briefly eclipse hunger. She said his name very softly, once, then again.

It was a strange moment for him to feel humble. He said huskily, "Such a gift you've given me, Jenessa."

"Oh, no, it's you—you're giving me myself."

Tenderness washed over him, as vast as the ocean and as mysterious. He made no attempt to hide it; wasn't sure he could. Tenderness was new to Bryce; as new as what Jenessa was experiencing in bed with him.

Again she thrust her body into his; his face convulsed, desire asserting its primitive claims. Touching her where she was most sensitive, watching the storm gather in her face, he waited until she was falling into its heart before he allowed himself to fall with her.

His cry mingled with hers, his inner convulsions mirroring her own. He collapsed on top of her, his harsh breathing stirring her hair. Against his rib cage he could feel the racing of her heart, an astonishing intimacy even after all they had shared. Putting his arms around her, he held her close; and knew in his heart he never wanted to let her go.

Bryce pushed that thought aside, as the tumult of release gradually quietened. Only then did he raise his head. "Next time," he said with a crooked grin, "I'll show a little more finesse."

"You were perfect," Jenessa said, her own smile so

radiant that his throat closed with emotion. "I can't tell you how happy I am that I waited for you."

And what was he to say to that? "I'm honored that you did," he said clumsily.

Tenderness, humility, honor...what was going on? Not that he was going to analyze it when Jenessa was lying so trustingly in his arms. So obviously happy.

"Your body is beautiful," she said, running her fingers along his shoulder to the pulse at the base of his throat.

His blood thickened. He said with an edge of laughter, "Unfortunately, making sure we don't start a baby means I have to head for the bathroom."

"But you'll come back."

"You've already persuaded me."

"I didn't do anything," she teased.

"You don't have to," he said, and eased free of her.

In the bathroom, Bryce looked at himself in the mirror for a long moment. He looked the same as he always did: eyes, mouth, nose and hair all in their accustomed places. But he didn't feel the same. He felt as though he'd been hit over the head with a baseball bat.

One woman had done that to him.

All I did was take Jenessa to bed, he told himself. How about I go back now, and do it again...and this time it'll be ordinary. Pleasurable, of course. But not earth-shattering.

She'd pulled the covers down in his absence, and was lying on the dark sheets, her body a flow of long, lissome curves. His groin stirred, his hunger unslaked. Then she opened her arms to him, a small gesture that tore through his defences. In a blur of movement he fell on the bed and pulled her hard against him. "God, how I want you," he muttered into her throat. Then he was kissing her as though they'd never kissed before.

This time Jenessa was more sure of herself, more sensual and more playful. Laughter mingled with their quickened breathing and their bodies' mounting passion; until, once again, they plummeted into the throb of release, that place of darkness and light, of a pleasure so sharp as to be almost painful.

Bryce lay very still. Ordinary? Nothing about Jenessa was ordinary. Nor was anything in his response. Earlier, he'd talked to her about his own risk in this affair he was embarking on. But had he meant it? Had he seriously considered that affairs by their very definition end? That the two people involved move on to other lovers, other beds?

He couldn't stand the thought of Jenessa in another man's arms.

She said softly, "You've gone away from me. What are you thinking about, Bryce?"

He'd always known she was astute. He looked up, smoothing her hair back from her face; her cheeks were delicately flushed. "I told you I'd be faithful to you," he said bluntly. "But I never thought to ask the same of you."

"It's not even an issue. Of course I will be." She bit her lip. "Until we go our separate ways."

"Don't let's talk about that. Not now."

"Sooner or later we'll have to."

"But not today." He smoothed the voluptuous curve of her lip with his finger. "I hate to sound so prosaic, and I know we ate lunch on the way, but I'm starving."

"Sex burns a lot of calories," she said, just as though she'd been doing it all her adult life.

They showered together, which took quite a while. Then they wandered hand in hand up to the main lodge in search of a snack. While they ate, Jenessa told him about the time she'd spent in New York with Leonora: how they'd gone to art galleries and to the studio where her mother taught modern dance; how they'd talked and talked, starting to bridge their long absence from each other; how they'd hugged each other at the station when Jenessa had left to come home. "I have you to thank,

Bryce,'' she concluded. ''If you hadn't sent me that video, I'd still be estranged from my mother.''

''You'd have done something about it yourself sooner or later,'' he said evenly.

''Later, maybe. Not sooner. Why do you have such a hard time accepting gratitude?''

Because it's another step toward an intimacy I can't handle. Bryce forced himself to smile. ''You're welcome,'' he said. Stroking her fingertips with lingering pleasure, he added, ''Finished? Shall we go back?''

Predictably, they made love before dinner. They also had a wild coupling in the middle of the night, and as a result were the last to arrive for breakfast. After breakfast, Jenessa fell asleep on the couch. Bryce sat in the chair across from her, ostensibly reading, in actuality gazing at her sleeping face as though it might give him some answers. Some clues as to what was going on. If this weekend had been intended to teach him more about her, it had succeeded, he thought. Her courage he'd never doubted. But her readiness to trust him, to expose her body's needs and vulnerabilities to him, were new.

He'd sworn off marriage long ago, partly because he'd seen the terrible damage it could inflict. And along with that had gradually hardened a resolve never to bring a child of his own into the world. He wasn't so naive as to think that all unions were like his parents'; or that there were no happy children. In the last year, Travis, Julie and now Samantha had given the lie to that. But commitment of any kind made him feel trapped. Caged. Caught.

Vulnerable.

He was glad when Jenessa woke up and expressed a wish to walk along the beach. When they returned, their jackets damp from the mist, she took out her painting gear, and three-quarters of an hour later said shyly, ''Want to see?''

In watercolors she'd painted beach and ocean, the sand disappearing into the sea, the sea vanishing in the mist.

No sharp edges, everything blending into everything else. He said, "That's how it feels when I'm in bed with you."

"So you understand."

"Would you give me that painting, Jenessa?"

"I was hoping you'd ask."

He said roughly, "We'll have to leave in a couple of hours. Come to bed with me before we go."

"I was hoping you'd ask that, too."

Their lovemaking was wild and tumultuous, as though they craved to imprint each other on their flesh. Afterward, spent in her arms, Bryce said, "I'm out of town again all week—in Texas and then Maryland. When I get back on Friday, can I come and stay overnight at your place?"

Underlying his request was the need to make love to her in her bed, on her territory. She said, fluttering her lashes at him, "You mean I have to wait that long?"

"I could stay in Wellspring all weekend. And I'll call you from Texas."

Her smile was brilliant. "Okay and okay," she said. Color rising in her cheeks, she added, "I know I have no basis for comparison. But you're the most wonderful lover I could possibly have asked for."

"And you're more than I could have imagined."

For a moment he thought he saw pain flicker across her features; but it was gone before he could be sure. Sitting up on the bed, she said lightly, "We're turning into a mutual admiration society. Who's first in the shower?"

Bryce stretched to his full length, yawning. "You are. I feel as lazy as all get-out."

"When your muscles move like that," she said rapidly, "I want to jump you. It's not decent. Not after what we just did."

"Friday's only five days away, Jenessa my darling."

Her lashes flickered. "Five days is one hundred and twenty hours," she said. "And I loathe cold showers."

She stalked toward the bathroom stark naked. Bryce

had already figured out that five days was about four too many; and only when he was in the tropics did he favor cold showers.

Texas and Maryland in July? Yeah, he could legitimately turn on the cold tap. The other thing he could do was check off the hours until he'd arrive at Jenessa's little house and fall into bed with her.

This weekend had only made him want her more.

CHAPTER ELEVEN

MONDAY morning found Jenessa face-to-face with a blank canvas.

Her mind was blank, too. Any sketches she'd done hadn't approximated the emotions seething in her body. The mother she'd never known, the lover she'd never had: those gaps in her psyche had now been replaced by Leonora's warm spirit, and Bryce's passion. When she closed her eyes, she could feel the strength of his arms about her body, and hear the huskiness in his deep voice just as if he were standing beside her.

He wasn't. He was on his way to Texas.

Instead, she was standing beside a canvas on which she ached to transfer in color, texture and form the huge shifts of the last few days.

Wing it, Jenessa.

She tried. Her palette rich with cadmium red and cobalt blue, with chrome yellow and the deepest of greens and purples, she did her best; but brush and knife, hand and eye wouldn't translate whatever it was she was so desperately seeking.

She was trying too hard.

She put some Mexican music on her CD player, danced around the room, laughed at herself because she had none of Leonora's fluidity, and tried again. Painting and over-painting, daubing and scraping, she gained the smallest of inklings of what she was searching for. But the rest of the canvas was a mess. Ninety-nine percent mess, she decided gloomily, realizing that her back was full of kinks and she was hungry.

118

She glanced at the clock. Four-thirty? It couldn't be. But it was.

No wonder she was hungry.

Yesterday morning Bryce had fed her slices of melon in bed, his fingers wet with juice, his gray eyes stormy. Bryce. Who had taken her body by storm and altered her unutterably.

Maybe she was as afraid of the power he had over her as she was of her aborted painting. She had allowed him to enter far more than her body; and she'd understood from the very beginning that at some point he would leave her. Not today. Not next week. But someday he would move on, to other women and to beds other than her own; and she would be alone as she'd never been before. To be alone when that was all she'd ever known had the familiarity of long experience. To be abandoned having known the bliss of intimacy: just thinking about it scared her to death.

She wasn't sure how she would bear it.

So what was she trying to paint? Passion or terror?

With an exclamation of disgust Jenessa cleaned her brushes, pulled a face at the canvas and stamped into the kitchen. Prepackaged macaroni and cheese, along with a salad from her garden, made her feel minimally better. She spent the evening baby-sitting for her friends Susan and David down the lane; three small boys under the age of ten were more than enough to keep her mind off abandonment, creativity and Bryce.

When she got home, there was a message on her voice mail. "If you get in before midnight, call me," Bryce said, and reeled off the number of his hotel room.

It was ten forty-eight. Quickly Jenessa hit the number keys, and then his voice surged over the line. "Bryce Laribee."

"I wish you were here," she said.

"Are you in bed?"

"Standing by the kitchen table."

"Have you ever made love on the kitchen floor?"

"You know I haven't. But I'm willing to try," she said. "Next weekend."

In a few very explicit sentences Bryce described exactly what he'd like to do to her. Her cheeks flaming, Jenessa said weakly, "I'd have to sweep the floor first...I'm not the best of housekeepers."

He laughed. "How big's your bed?"

"Plenty big for you and me."

"This has turned into an obscene phone call."

"Another first," she said demurely.

"I fly in midafternoon on Friday. Why don't you make a reservation for dinner someplace near you?"

"I already have."

"Good food?" he asked sceptically.

"The very best...the chef's a blonde."

"You're supposed to be painting. Not cooking."

"Don't even mention painting," she said darkly. "How were your meetings?"

They talked for another half an hour, then Bryce said abruptly, "You'd better get some sleep. Get lots of sleep this week, Jenessa."

Her knees felt weak and she ached with longing. "I'm going to end this conversation the way I began it," she said. "I wish you were here."

"I will be. It can't be soon enough. 'Bye." The connection was cut.

It can't be soon enough. Those weren't the words of a man intent on leaving her.

Hugging to herself the timbre of his voice and the seductive images he'd conjured in her mind, she went to bed. Bryce phoned her again on Wednesday. Although she did her regular stint at the shelter, and went for a swim at the pool on Thursday afternoon, Jenessa spent hours in the studio that week. She made several promising starts, only to have them founder before they had the potential to satisfy her. On Thursday evening she talked to Leonora, whose advice, not surprisingly, was to persevere: and when Jenessa felt really defeated, to take a deep breath and persevere some more.

"Thanks a lot," Jenessa said wryly.

"My pleasure. And I mean that literally. It is such a pleasure to talk to you, Jenessa."

"And for me. To talk to you," Jenessa said incoherently but with real sincerity.

"May I ask you something? Did you thank Bryce for sending the video?"

"Oh. Yes. I did."

"Good. You might want to persevere there, too. You'll never be satisfied with anyone facile."

"That word does not apply to Bryce Laribee," Jenessa said vigorously.

"My mistake when I was young was to interpret Charles's dynamism for depth."

"So Bryce has both...that's what you're saying?"

"Depth. And darkness, too."

Jenessa shivered. "I should go, Leonora." After they'd said their goodbyes, Jenessa rang off, then walked into the studio, where she lined up her four canvasses in a row. Too much raw color. Altogether too hectic, she thought, her eyes narrowed. Tomorrow she'd try for darkness, and perhaps that would take her where she needed to go.

In the early morning light, she worked like a woman possessed. Blue black, ebony black and lamp black swirled onto the canvas in a chaotic blend of shadows backlit with streaks of white and a lurid scarlet that looked like blood. Abruptly Jenessa put down her brush and stared at the canvas. Black, white and red: she'd produced an artistic cliché, she thought, near despair. What in heck had she been thinking of? And what would she title it? Struggle To Approximate Emotions Not Yet Understood? Or, more tritely, Work in Progress?

Despite the cliché, she was—maybe—one small step closer to an unknown destination.

Leaving the canvas full in the light, feeling tired and strangely vulnerable, Jenessa went out into the garden. Weeding, as always, soothed her. The crop of beets she'd planted to replace those Bryce had pulled up were flourishing. He'd be here tonight. In her bed.

Where he belonged.

Her fingers stilled. Yes, he belonged in her bed. But only temporarily, she mustn't forget that. For Leonora was right. He was a man of darkness, and many secrets. None of which he planned to share with her.

By the time five o'clock on Friday afternoon rolled around, Jenessa was in a fine state of nerves. What if she and Bryce couldn't recapture the bliss they'd found in each other's arms last weekend? What if he'd spent the week in the company of sophisticated and sexy businesswomen who knew the score and thought affairs were the only way to go? What if her inexperience no longer charmed him?

She wasn't an urban sophisticate. She was a struggling artist who'd buried herself in the country.

An artist, moreover, who was no longer in control of her life. She'd let Bryce into it, whereupon any illusion of control had vanished.

Chewing on her lip, Jenessa added a few last minute touches to the dinner table, which was set in the screened porch. The porch overlooked the garden; it was hung with grapevines that kept the air cool and tinged the shadows with gold and green. The pasta sauce had turned out perfectly, her salad was made entirely from her garden, and she'd produced a chocolate mousse as smooth as velvet. She was wearing her flowered skirt and halter top, her hair pulled into a knot on the top of her head, curls teasing her nape. What if Bryce had an accident on the way? What if his plane had crashed?

What if she'd run out of things to paint?

With an impatient exclamation Jenessa poured herself a glass of wine. A car pulled into her driveway, the tires crunching in the gravel.

Her heart racing, she hurried to the front door. Bryce was taking the steps two at a time, his jacket slung over his arm, his tie loose, an overnight bag in one hand and a great sheaf of deep pink roses in the other. As Jenessa walked out onto the verandah, he looked up and stopped in his tracks. "Each time I see you, you're more beautiful," he said.

Her worries dropped from her shoulders as if they'd never been; the look in his eyes alone would have reassured her that she was both desired and desirable. "Roses," she said. "Lots and lots of roses."

"Yeah...I know you've got a garden full of them. But they reminded me of the color of your cheeks after we make love."

She held the door open. "Then I can scarcely say they're pretty, can I?"

He walked inside, dumped his bag on the floor, his jacket and the roses on the nearest chair, and took her in his arms. His kiss was lengthy, thorough and passionate. With a deep sigh of repletion Jenessa said, "I was afraid you might not want me anymore."

"I want you entirely too much. As I'm sure you can tell." He grinned at her, his teeth very white. "But first I need a shower and a shave—I didn't bother going home, just drove straight from the airport. A glass of wine would go down okay, too."

"You can have whatever you want," she said with a sly grin.

He nuzzled his face into her throat. "You smell delicious. Have we got time for you to show me how big the bed is before dinner?"

"We've got all weekend," she said, her laugh a cascade of pure happiness. "The bathroom's this way. Let me get you some towels, then I'll pour your wine."

He yanked his tie off, tossing it on top of his jacket. "You could kiss me again first."

"Another kiss like the last one and I won't be able to find the bathroom, let alone the towels."

"We'll risk it," Bryce muttered, and closed his mouth over hers.

She was trembling when he released her; the pulse in the V of his shirt was throbbing against his skin. "Who needs wine when you're here?" he said, grabbed his leather toilet kit from his bag and headed for the bathroom.

A foolish smile plastered to her face, Jenessa put the roses in a vase and poured a second glass of wine, then carried both glasses into her bedroom. The water was running in the shower. After taking off all her clothes, she put on Bryce's jacket and tie. Then, arranging herself on the bed in a pose worthy of a centerfold, she stuck one of the pink roses behind her ear.

Bryce walked into the bedroom, his hips swathed in a white towel. Laughter lines creasing his eyes, he said, "You look ten times better in that jacket than I do. The rose is a nice touch."

"I'm glad you like it."

"It's not all I like," he said roughly. "I want your hair loose, Jenessa."

She sat up, slipped off his jacket and took the pins from her hair, her breasts bouncing gently as she moved. In the soft light of evening, her skin was pale as ivory, smooth as rose petals. Shaking her hair free, she held out her arms. "Come here, Bryce."

He fell on her like an eagle on its prey. But Jenessa matched him kiss for kiss, caress for caress, as wild and imperious as an eagle herself. Their climax was explosive;

scarcely able to breathe, Jenessa clung to him as though she was drowning and he was her lifeline.

His breath was sobbing in his throat. "My God, woman," he gasped, "what did you do to me?"

She could scarcely find her voice, let alone think of anything to say. "It's a good thing supper's already made," she croaked. "I'm not sure I can stand up."

Reaching over her, the heat of his skin brushing her rib cage, he passed her a glass of wine, then picked up his own. "To weekends," he said.

"To us," she responded, her chin high.

Points of fire in his irises, Bryce said, "To the most beautiful woman in the world."

"To the sexiest man."

He said flatly, "This isn't just about sex, Jenessa. Us, I mean."

She wouldn't have expected him to say that. Her throat tight, she muttered, "No. It's not."

"But don't ask me what it is about."

He was restlessly moving his bare shoulders in a way that both entranced and frightened her. "I think we should eat," she said, and swung her legs over the side of the bed.

It was one of those meals where everything turned out perfectly. They ate by candlelight, the scents of the garden drifting through the screen, the faraway hooting of a barred owl punctuating their conversation. After lingering over coffee, they washed the dishes; in the midst of this domestic task, Jenessa reached around Bryce for a saucepan, he grabbed her by the hip and suddenly they were making love against the refrigerator door.

Her arms around his neck, happiness flooding her veins, Jenessa said, "Better than the kitchen floor."

"I'm saving that for tomorrow."

She buried her face in his shoulder. "I'm so glad you're

here, Bryce,'' she said in a muffled voice. ''I missed you. All week I felt like I'd been locked in a room without paper or pencils or paint. As though part of me was missing.''

Abruptly he moved away from her, straightening her skirt. ''Maybe we should go to bed. And this time, go to sleep.''

''Did I say something I shouldn't?''

''Hell, Jenessa, I don't know! Just don't—I don't even want to go there. Let's go to bed, it's late.''

''I won't hide my feelings from you, Bryce—they're part of me.''

''I'm not asking you to. But be careful, that's all I'm saying.''

He was being punctilious about protection; they were certainly being careful that way. But how could she protect herself against her own heart? Wishing she'd kept her mouth shut, Jenessa wiped the counter, then went to the bathroom. When she came out, wearing her least unsexy nightgown because she'd forgotten to iron her silk pyjamas, Bryce was already in bed.

He looked very much at home, the sheets partway up his chest. As she climbed in beside him, he took her in his arms. His breath ruffling her hair, he said forcefully, ''This is all so new, Jenessa. To both of us. We knew before we started that any relationship between us wouldn't be casual. But it's so far from casual that I'm way off balance. So bear with me, okay?''

''Okay,'' she said; and five minutes later was fast asleep.

Bryce woke around three in the morning. He lay still in the unfamiliar bed, listening to Jenessa's soft breathing. In her sleep she'd curled against him, her spine pressed into his chest, her thighs warm against his legs. His arm had fallen across her hip. He was in fine shape to make love to her right now, he thought ruefully. For the third time in less than twelve hours.

Would he ever get enough of her?

Easing away from her, he gazed into the darkness. Jenessa lived on a back lane in a small village. The only light was that of the stars; far away in the trees, the owl was still hooting. Maybe he should have thought twice— or three times—before embarking on this affair. Jenessa wasn't like the other women he'd known, easy come and easy go. She was vulnerable, capable of depths of feeling that scared the living daylights out of him.

Not a comfortable thought. Not for a man whose parents' marriage had been a walking disaster; and who knew firsthand the pain of abandonment.

Half an hour later, wide awake, Bryce slid out of bed. Hauling on his briefs, he went to the bathroom. Then, on his way back to the bedroom, on an impulse he didn't understand, he put his head in the studio door.

Half a dozen easels, five of them holding paintings. Carefully he felt for the light switch. Blinking against the brightness, his eyes swept over four abstracts vivid with color to find the painting that stood full under the skylight. His heart contracted. Suddenly cold, he wrapped his arms around his chest, his head hunched into his shoulders. For the space of a full minute he stood there, like someone waiting for the next blow.

How could oil paint slapped on canvas affect him so deeply? The whirling shadows Jenessa had depicted captured his childish terror of living with a man who could explode into violence at any moment and for no reason that a little boy could grasp. The streaks of red—oh, those were easy, Bryce thought grimly. Fletcher liked to draw blood. As for the ghostly trails of white, stark against the shadows, weren't they his mother? She'd had a smile as bright as daylight, he remembered that. But hadn't Fletcher turned her into a wraith of herself?

The ghosts of his past, he thought with a shudder, pain clenching his gut, called up by the woman he was sleeping with. Coincidence or not, could Jenessa possibly know that much about him?

It was as if the secrets he'd been guarding for so many years were no longer his.

CHAPTER TWELVE

BEHIND him the faintest of sounds made Bryce whirl, his pulse racing. Jenessa was standing in the open doorway, her hand on the frame, her features blurred with sleep. "I woke up and I didn't know where you were," she faltered.

He looked at her in silence, his fists bunched at his sides. Of all the emotions boiling in his chest, anger was uppermost; within a split second his decision was made. He had to tell her everything, even if it meant his long-held defences would crumble as if they'd never existed. The words spilling out of him, he snarled, "I never told you a single goddamn thing about the way I grew up— what are you, a witch?"

She flinched, her shocked gaze going from him to the canvas. "I just—"

"You got it all. The fear. The violence. The drinking, the shouting and cursing. The way she stayed with that bastard, day after day, month after month."

"What bastard?" Jenessa whispered.

"My father. Of course."

He suddenly turned his back on the painting; he couldn't stand to look at it anymore. "My father," he repeated, advancing on her. "Fletcher Laribee. He's one reason I'll never marry. Let alone have any children of my own."

Jenessa stood her ground. Although her chin was high, her cheeks, Bryce noticed distantly, were as ghostly white as the streaks in her painting. "What did he do, Bryce?" she asked. "And what happened to your mother?"

"Who, Rose? Oh, she left. Dumped me at a woman's shelter and never came back for me. Must have forgotten

129

she had a kid.'' His laugh was like a fist shattering glass. ''She's the other reason I'm not into commitment. I thought she loved me. I know I loved her. But she walked out the door and never came back.''

''So you decided you'd never love anyone else,'' Jenessa said in a dazed voice.

''When they went looking for my dad, he'd gone, too. Vanished without a trace. Who knows? Maybe she went with him. Figured they were better off without me.''

Blindly Jenessa reached out for him, but Bryce took a sharp step back; her outstretched hand fell to her side. ''How did you manage to paint all that?'' he demanded. ''How in God's name did you know? Have I been babbling in my sleep?''

''No! I wasn't painting you, Bryce. It just happened...I went where the brush took me.''

''It looks as if you know me better than I know myself,'' he said harshly.

And he hated her for it, Jenessa thought with an inward shudder. Wishing she'd turned the painting to the wall rather than leaving it where it would be the first thing anyone would see when they walked into the studio, she said carefully, ''Your father was a violent man?''

''You could say so. If beating up on my mother is what you call violent. Probably raping her, too, although I was too young to figure that one out.''

With an effort Jenessa kept her voice steady. ''Did he hit you, too?''

''Just enough to keep me out from underfoot. I was only four when they both took off. Too little to defend my mum, but old enough to live in constant fear. Sober, he wasn't too bad. But drunk he was mean as a cut cat. That's why you'll never catch me having more than a couple of beers.''

Too shocked to be tactful, Jenessa blurted, ''You're afraid you'll turn out like him?''

''Why wouldn't I—I've got his genes, he fathered me.

You think I'd ever inflict that kind of terror on a kid of mine? Better not to have the kid in the first place."

"Bryce, I've never seen a trace of that kind of violence in you. Not once!"

Now that he'd started, Bryce couldn't seem to stop. "About a month after I turned four, my dad got royally drunk. Came bursting through the door and went for my mum. I picked up the truck I was playing with, rusted metal and sharp edges, and bashed him on the leg as hard as I could. He threw me clear across the room and when I came to, my mum was lying on the floor, bleeding, and he'd gone...later that day she took me to the shelter."

"Didn't the police ever come?"

Bryce said cynically, "The people who lived in those streets weren't in the habit of calling the police. And if they did, it'd just go down on the books as one more domestic incident. There were a lot of those, and only so many cops."

"So you were alone. No one to turn to."

"I'm not asking you to feel sorry for me," he said sharply. "I never had any intention of telling you this, you know that as well as I do. But when I saw that painting, it all—anyway, now you understand why marriage is a dirty word to me. Always will be."

"Children of abusive parents don't necessarily turn out to be abusive," she said fiercely. "Haven't you read any of the research?"

"What I know, I know in my blood," he retorted. "I don't need the jargon that a bunch of academics can cook up."

"Then you're the one who's stuck," Jenessa said.

She hadn't meant to say that. Her chin a notch higher, she waited for his response.

His breath hissed between his teeth; his fists were still clenched at his sides. He said, "Aren't you afraid to be alone in the house with me, Jenessa?"

"No. I'm not."

"What if I took it in my head to finish off that bottle of wine? To start on the next one? Then what would you do?"

"That's a rhetorical question. Because it's not going to happen."

"You're very sure of yourself."

"I'm the one who painted the picture."

"So we're back where we began," he said in an ugly voice.

"You're cold," she said quietly. "Let's go to bed."

Deep lines had carved themselves from his nostrils to the corners of his mouth. His eyes were like a winter sky, and with every line of his body he was repudiating her. "I'm going to stay up for a while. You go to bed."

"I'm not going without you."

"Then it'll be a long night."

For a moment she quailed. Who was she, to break through the barriers of a lifetime? Barriers she more than understood now. She said implacably, "You have to believe that the painting has nothing to do with your past. But it will never be shown, or sold. I promise. Because it's not finished."

"You could have fooled me," Bryce grated, wondering where she was going with this, wishing she'd leave him alone.

"It's a work in progress," she said dryly. "Which is what we are. You and me."

"We're having an affair, that's all!"

"We're in so deep we're changing each other."

"Speak for yourself," he rasped.

She tossed her head, her hair rippling in the light. "Why haven't you ever made any attempt to trace your mother? Or your father?"

"What would I do that for?"

"For the same reason that you sent me that video of Leonora...to deal with a past that's holding you hostage."

"You've been reading too much pop psychology," he

sneered; and with a distant part of his brain knew he was behaving reprehensibly.

"I'm regaining the mother I never knew because of you," Jenessa said evenly. "Now it's your turn. You know her name, the dates, the name of the shelter. Go find your mother, Bryce. Talk to her. Turn her into a real person. If you dare."

He took a single step toward her. "Watch what you're saying."

She held her ground. "I'm not afraid of you. Can't you tell? I don't believe you'd ever turn your fists on me."

"You're far too trusting."

"I've made love with you," she flashed. "You think that doesn't teach me a whole lot about you?"

She wasn't quite as calm as she was pretending to be; beneath the thin fabric of her nightgown, her breast was rising and falling; her jawline was tense. He said irritably, "Did a maiden aunt give you that nightgown?"

"You could buy me a new one," she said. "If you want to."

His heart clenched as though a fist was squeezing it. This was the moment of choice. To stay with her or to leave. That was what she meant.

"You've got guts," he said hoarsely, "I'll give you that."

"You're worth fighting for."

And how was he supposed to respond to that particular statement? Wishing he could force himself to close the distance between them and take her in his arms, Bryce said woodenly, "You don't know what you're talking about."

"I'm going to tell you something I've never told anyone," she flared. "I know it doesn't compare to what happened to you—but it's the reason I stay away from my father. One evening, when I was about seven, I was dancing all by myself by the lilac bushes on Manatuck...pretending I was a princess, or a beautiful white swan. My father came 'round the corner and saw me. He picked me up and shook me as though I was a rag doll, I had bruises on my arms for days afterward. His eyes were crazed...then he froze and dropped me, and in a voice that cut like a knife he told me never to dance again or he wouldn't be responsible for the consequences.''

"Son of a bitch," Bryce said. He could see the scene as clearly as if she'd painted it: the innocent little girl with her long blond hair, twirling to her own music; and the man who'd done his best to destroy her.

Her voice broke. "He never loved me for what I was. He only wanted me to be someone else. Someone, I see now, who was like Corinne—not like Leonora. But Leonora was my mother!''

Without even stopping to think, Bryce strode toward her and enfolded her in his arms. He pressed her face to his bare chest, wishing he'd been there to protect her, knowing at the same time the futility of such a wish. She was trembling very lightly. He picked her up with an exaggerated grunt, hoping to make her smile. "If your feet are as cold as mine, we're in big trouble.''

"My heart feels cold," she said so quietly he could scarcely hear her. "Can you warm that, Bryce?''

He looked her full in the face and in a raw voice spoke the only truth he knew. "I don't know.''

"We could start with our feet," she replied, giving him a tiny smile.

The emotion flooding his chest was new to him. Not in the mood to analyze it, Bryce carried her into the bedroom. Once they were in bed, he flung his thigh over hers, pulled her into his body and held her close. But when he closed his eyes, all he could see was that ugly little apartment with its dirty windows and battered furniture. As a child he hadn't judged it; it had been home. Now, with hindsight, he recognized a poverty that went far beyond money.

It was a long time before he went to sleep again.

* * *

Once again, on Monday morning Jenessa was in her studio. Bryce had left the evening before to drive back to Boston. She arranged the silver tubes of paint on the table, her mind a long way away, and sighed, gazing out the window.

By Saturday morning, Bryce's revelations in the middle of the night had vanished as though they'd never happened. A couple of times she'd caught herself wondering if she'd dreamed them; and then assured herself she hadn't. When she'd reopened the topic of his childhood the next morning, suggesting he might want to go to social services and see what he could find out about his parents, he'd said in a voice of steel, "Jenessa, I don't want to talk about it. I should never have told you."

"But you did."

"If I hadn't come face-to-face with that painting in the middle of the night, I wouldn't have."

"Bryce, you told me I needed to build some bridges with my family. For my own sake. Wouldn't you be better off knowing what happened to your mother and father?"

"No."

And that had been the end of any conversation of depth between them. Sure, they'd had a good time the rest of the weekend, eating lunch in Masefield, working in the garden, making love with pleasure and inventiveness. But, for her at least, a shadow had lain across her happiness. The shadow of Bryce's past.

Because of his past, Bryce would never get married. Hence, she thought with an unhappy twist of her lips, this affair.

She could always end it. Before she got in too deep.

She didn't want to.

So that was that.

Jenessa worked hard all day, with results that left her in a foul mood. She was beginning to hate that nasty little word *stuck*. Hate it with a passion. What was wrong with her that she couldn't quit wasting her money and her time lathering canvasses with paint, only to end up with something that looked awful?

She could always sell it at the local craft shop, she thought grouchily. Although her gallery wouldn't think much of that plan. She knew what she needed. She needed Bryce Laribee to walk in the door right now and make mad, passionate love to her for at least three hours.

He hadn't phoned to let her know he got home safely last night, and he hadn't phoned yet this evening. Damn him anyway. She didn't need him. Not for making love and not for anything else.

Stuck. Treading water. Spinning her wheels. Jenessa looked up a number in her address book, picked up the phone, then put it down again. Was she really going to do this?

Or was she clean crazy?

Two days later, after a four-hour shift at the shelter, Jenessa was standing in the tree-lined mall of one of Boston's most fashionable streets. Across the road was the 19th century mansion that belonged to her father. It was solid and imposing, with ranks of bay windows whose flower boxes trailed ivy and perfectly groomed geraniums. Roses nodded against the mellow brick. Corinne's touch, she thought absently.

Charles was expecting her. She couldn't stand here like a statue for the next half hour.

She crossed the street and pressed the brass bell, the scent of the roses filling her nostrils. Charles opened the door. "Jenessa," he said heartily, "come in. Corinne's out, we've got the place to ourselves. Let me get you something to drink."

He led her past a formal living room, where she had a quick glimpse of her painting hanging prominently over a grand piano, into a drawing room that overlooked the back garden; it was a haven of shade and color. Then he started fussing with a tray of drinks. She said, "A glass of ice water would be lovely. It's really hot outside."

"Fine, fine." He disappeared for a couple of minutes, coming back with a frosted crystal glass of water. The ice bumped gently against the glass as he passed it to her. "I'm pleased to see you," he said.

On the bus, Jenessa had carefully rehearsed what she wanted to say; she was going to be cool, calm and collected, stating her case with impartial precision. She met her father's eyes, remembered as if it were yesterday that night by the lilacs, and said tautly, "Are you? Are you really?"

He laughed uneasily. "Why wouldn't I be? After all, you're my daughter."

His response only fueled her anger. "I'm Leonora's daughter as well. But you never wanted me to be her daughter. Do you remember the evening you found me near the lilacs at Castlereigh? How you picked me up and shook me, threatened me, terrified me out of my wits? Just because I was dancing."

"You took me by surprise that evening. All I ever heard from your mother was dancing, dancing, dancing. Do you wonder I reacted the way I did?"

"I was seven years old!"

"Old enough to know better."

Sheer fury loosed Jenessa's tongue. "You wanted a carbon copy of yourself—that's why you enrolled me in business college when I finished high school, without even consulting me to see what I wanted. I'd scraped through arithmetic all the way through school—what were you thinking of?"

"The arts pay extremely badly," Charles said stiffly. "I'd have been a poor father had I encouraged you to go to art school."

"I went anyway."

"You always were headstrong."

"If I hadn't been, you'd have destroyed me," she retorted. "Shaped me into something I wasn't and didn't want to be. Is that what being a good father means to you?"

Her voice had risen. He rapped, "Why are you dragging this up now?"

"I'd have been better off without a father!"

He slammed his glass down on a side table with scant regard for the crystal or the polished wood. "How can you say such a thing?"

"Very easily. You lied to me about my mother, letting me grow up thinking she was dead. And then you did your best to kill anything in me that might remind you of the woman who ran away from you. Come on, Charles—for once, tell the truth! You hated Leonora for what she did to you. You didn't want to admit to your fancy friends that you couldn't keep your wife. So you exiled my mother and deceived your three children. And all out of pride. Out of a fear of what people might think." Her shoulders slumped. "I'll never understand you. So how can I possibly forgive you?"

"It wasn't pride!"

"Of course it was. Leonora stopped loving you. She defied you. She made a fool of you. So you buried her as if she'd never been."

"All right," Charles said, jamming his hands in his pockets, "there was a measure of pride in my decision. But it was more than pride. Far more. I loved her. Adored her. Worshiped the ground she walked on. I did from the first moment I saw her...I couldn't help myself. So within days of meeting her I took her to bed, Travis was conceived and we married. Then she was mine. Only mine."

"She was another possession," Jenessa said in a dazed voice.

"You're far too intelligent to say something so simplistic. Possessions can be replaced. If something's flawed, you throw it away and buy a new one, a better one, a perfect one. But Leonora was all I ever wanted! And I lost her."

"You drove her away," Jenessa said.

"I never really had her," Charles said in a low voice. "I knew that from the beginning—that something in her would always elude me. Her essence. The mystery that made her a dancer."

"That was why you hated me dancing?"

"You try living with someone you can never entirely possess," he said with a depth of bitterness that horrified Jenessa. "Knowing in your heart that nothing you can possibly do will open her innermost core to you. It was hell, pure hell."

Bryce, Jenessa thought, stupefied. *That's what it's like for me when I'm with Bryce. He's refusing to share himself with me. To commit to anything other than the temporary.*

But her father was still speaking. "I was a fool back then," he said caustically. "I thought if I prevented her from dancing as much as possible, kept her away from her artistic, bohemian friends, everything would be all right. I smothered her with houses and jewels and money, I built Castlereigh for her, took her to Europe and the Bahamas, and I thought she'd be content. Settle down. Stay with me forever…"

"But you were wrong," Jenessa said quietly. "All you did was drive her away."

"That's right. I came home from a business trip and found her letter telling me she was flying to Paris to study avant garde dance." Briefly he closed his eyes. "The paper she'd written on smelled of her perfume."

Bryce's skin...wouldn't she know the elusive, masculine scent of him anywhere? "So you exiled her."

"I was torn apart by grief. By despair. By rage at myself for my stupidity and rage at her for leaving me. Out of my mind? Oh, yes, I was out of my mind. So I faked a funeral, told everyone—including Travis—that she'd died, and put the lawyers onto her so that she'd never dare show her face on this side of the Atlantic again."

To her horror, Jenessa saw tears trickle down his cheeks. As she made an instinctive move toward him, Charles added in a muffled voice, "It was a wicked thing to do. I see that now. Travis made me see it. And that's why, in the only way I know how, I've been trying to connect with you, Jenessa. Brent and I have always been close. But not you and I."

Impulsively Jenessa rested her hands on his shoulders, looking up into his ravaged face. "I never knew you had this much emotion in you," she whispered. "Except for that one time by the lilacs, you were always so cold, so much in control."

Clumsily Charles put his arms around her. "I'm sorry, Jenessa. More sorry than I can say for what I did to you. Because you're right, I was trying to kill your mother in you. I couldn't bear to be reminded of her."

"But you love Corinne...don't you?"

"Yes, I love Corinne. She's been good for me—and did her best to be good to you. She's not an effusive woman, but in her way she loves you."

Jenessa knew he was right. She could have asked if he still loved Leonora; and decided not to. That was between himself and her mother. It was enough that they could meet socially, be together at family gatherings. Her vision blurred with tears, she said, "I'm sorry I yelled at you.

But I'm not sorry you told me all this. It's overdue. Long overdue.''

"I don't know if you can ever forgive me. I robbed you of your mother, and that was a terrible thing to do. And yet, in a twisted way, I did it out of love. Because I do love you, I want you to know that.''

Jenessa looked up, scrubbing at her wet cheeks. "I've forgiven you already,'' she said with a shaky smile, "and I love you, too, Dad.'' Then she watched as two more tears spilled from his eyes.

"Love and forgiveness,'' he said heavily. "That's more than I deserve.''

"I'm so glad you have one of my paintings in the house. Would you let me paint one for Castlereigh?''

"I'd be honored,'' Charles said, standing a little taller.

"I'll do it,'' she promised. "Do you know what? I'd like a glass of wine. Let's toast a new beginning.''

"Champagne,'' Charles said. "Nothing but the best. I'll be right back.''

She watched him leave. If someone had told her that such a capacity for emotion was locked within her father, she'd have laughed at them. Laughed and disbelieved. Nothing could alter the harm he'd done to his first wife and his children; but now she understood why, and had seen for herself his bitter regret and his need to be reconciled with his only daughter.

A few minutes later Charles came back, dusting off a venerable bottle of champagne. After he'd popped the cork, they raised their glasses. "To my daughter,'' Charles said gruffly, "who is her own woman.''

A lump in her throat, Jenessa drank. By mutual consent they began talking about lighter matters. An hour later Jenessa said, "I'm going to head home, Dad, I'd like to get an early start in the studio tomorrow. Give Corinne my love. I'll call her and we'll arrange a dinner date very soon.''

"We'd like that,'' Charles said. ''In the meantime, let me drive you to the bus station.''

"I'll take the subway,'' Jenessa said. ''It'll give me time for my thoughts to settle. But thanks for the offer.''

She gave her father a fierce hug at the front door. Then, oblivious to the heat, she walked along the elegant row of town houses in the shade of the trees. But when she got to the subway, impulsively she took the red line, getting off at the station nearest to Beacon Hill. She should phone first. But something stopped her. Walking the few blocks to Bryce's house, she climbed the steps and rang the bell.

CHAPTER THIRTEEN

WHEN the doorbell chimed, Bryce was about to leave for his sports club; he ran downstairs in his shorts and T-shirt, his bag in one hand, and checked through the peephole. Distorted by the glass, he saw the woman who was haunting him, night and day; it was as though his dreams had conjured her up. Quickly he opened the door.

"Oh," Jenessa said, "you were about to go out...I should have phoned."

"I can go later—I was planning on jogging on an air-conditioned track rather than on the street. Come in. I didn't know you were coming into town today."

"I didn't know myself." Once inside, she positioned herself near the door and said rapidly, "I've just been to see Charles." Gathering momentum as she went, she described their meeting, and all that she'd learned. Then she said with a radiant smile, "So I've forgiven him. I'm not angry with him anymore. I can't tell you how wonderful that feels, Bryce. It's as though I've put down a burden I've been carrying for a long time." She laughed. "I feel light enough to dance just like my mother."

His brain working overtime, Bryce asked, "And you came straight here to tell me?"

Taken aback, she said, "Of course. It's hugely important...surely you understand that."

He understood too much. That Jenessa was willing to share her whole life with him, with all its crises and joys: something he wasn't willing to reciprocate. Yet every time he saw her, he was getting more deeply embroiled. When he thought of ending their affair before she got hurt, every cell in his body urged him not to be a fool; the prospect

143

of another man replacing him in her bed flooded him with jealousy.

But he couldn't—wouldn't—commit to her.

The silence had gone on too long. Jenessa said in a brittle voice, "I shouldn't have come. You don't want to hear about Charles and me. You just want me in your bed. Everything temporary and on the surface."

"I don't know what I want!"

She'd gone very pale. "A canvas is a surface. But there's no point putting paint on it unless the result says something about what's going on underneath. Brings the hidden and the unknown into the open."

"I know what you're asking," Bryce said tightly, "and the answer's no—I haven't made any attempt to find my mother or father."

"I've changed since we met," Jenessa cried. "But if you won't change, too, we can't go anywhere."

"Just where are we supposed to be going?"

She winced as though he'd struck her. "Nothing stands still," she said passionately. "Human beings, gardens, time itself...to be static is to die."

"You're quite the philosopher."

"Go to hell, Bryce Laribee!"

She looked angry enough to banish him there single-handed. And why wouldn't she, when with one hand he pulled her close and with the other pushed her away?

Trapped, he thought. They were both trapped. "Let's go upstairs," he said hoarsely. "I need to hold you and touch you, Jenessa. I don't know what's real anymore—except for you."

For a moment he thought she was going to refuse, and his heart froze in his chest. "Okay," she said.

Relief swamping him, he said bitterly, "You're braver than I am. Your mother and your father—you went looking for both of them."

"In retrospect, it wasn't that difficult. But, Bryce, when you go in search of your parents, you're venturing into the unknown—you have no idea where they are or what they've turned into. You're also reopening terrible memories. It's not the same at all.''

Hadn't his whole life been fashioned around avoiding that mean little apartment where Fletcher and Rose had entangled their lives? His money, his women, his many successes, weren't they all barricades against memory?

He dumped his bag on the floor, took Jenessa into his arms and pressed his face into the sweetly scented mass of her hair. She was his only certainty, he thought dimly. When he was holding her, he knew who he was.

A week later, in a light rain that slicked the dirt to the streets, Bryce was standing outside an old tenement house gazing up at the blank windows. He'd come directly here from the shelter where thirty-two years ago his mother had walked out the door and never come back.

Left him as though he was of as much value as a sack of potatoes.

At the shelter, they hadn't been able to tell him anything about his mother or his father; their records didn't go back that far. But the elderly janitor had suggested he seek out an old woman called Maybelline Parker, who'd been working night shifts during the time Bryce's mother would have stayed there.

Maybelline Parker lived in this building. If she couldn't tell him anything, he'd reached a dead end.

Is that what he wanted?

Bryce took the rickety stairs two at a time; he'd phoned her from the shelter, so she knew he was coming. When he tapped on a door that had a brave coat of red paint on it, the old woman who opened it had a smile as welcoming as the door. ''Well now,'' she said comfortably, ''haven't you grown into a fine-looking man?''

He had to smile back. In one quick glance he saw that Maybelline Parker's living room had very little of monetary value in it; but it was clean and orderly, china dogs crowding every surface, photos of soap opera stars pinned carefully to the faded wallpaper. She shuffled over to the stove; her purple-flowered housedress clashed with her green apron and her electric blue slippers, while her hair was pure white.

"You'll have a cup of tea, won't you, Mr. Laribee? Then we'll have a nice chat."

"The name's Bryce and I'd love one," he said, watching in some dismay as she threw enough tea bags in the pot to stun a horse.

"You just hitch that cat onto the floor, he takes up more room than I do."

The cat, who was fat and fluffy, lashed its enormous tail and eyed him balefully. Bryce, no coward, said, "That's okay, I'll sit on this other chair," and hitched out a wooden chair from the little table by the window. African violets, lovingly tended, were lined up on the sill.

The tea had sufficient caffeine to keep him awake all week; Maybelline put a plate of chocolate cookies in front of him and helped herself. "So you're Bryce...looks like you turned out real well. I'm glad for that."

"I've done okay," he said in magnificent understatement. "But the time's come when I need to find out about my parents. All I know is their names. Rose and Fletcher. And that she left me at the shelter, and he disappeared around the same time. Not much to go on."

Maybelline frowned at him in puzzlement. "That's all you know?" she repeated. "That your mom left you at the shelter?"

"I said it wasn't much to go on."

"They never told you anything more than that?"

It was his turn to frown. "No...should they have?"

She answered his question with one of her own. "You got a reason for looking for them?"

Maybe it was the tea scalding his throat that loosed his tongue. "I've never married," he said evenly, "and I decided long ago not to bring a kid into the world—"

He broke off, in a flash of insight suddenly understanding that the school he was planning to build was for a surrogate family: the boys and girls who went there would be the children he'd never have.

Abruptly he realized Maybelline was talking. "So you've met yourself a woman," she said. "She good enough for you?"

"You cut to the chase," he answered wryly.

"You didn't come here to talk about the weather."

"Yeah, she's more than good enough. But I saw what marriage did to my parents...I guess I'm afraid I'll turn out like my old man."

"You got a drinking problem?" Only with your tea, Bryce thought, and shook his head. "You push this woman around?"

He laughed. "I wouldn't want to try...I've never in my life raised a hand to a woman."

"Don't see what you're worrying 'bout, then."

"He was my father! His blood runs in mine, he was a drunk who could be as ugly as a starving dog."

"I got a good feeling 'bout you the minute you walked in my door," Maybelline said. "But I can set your mind to rest right easy on one score. Fletcher Laribee wasn't your dad."

Bryce almost choked on a mouthful of tea. "*What* did you say?"

"He moved in with Rose after she was widowed. She was already pregnant with you at the time. Your dad worked in the shipyards, his name was Neil Bryce Jackson and he was killed by one of them derricks. Came from out Iowa way as I recall."

"Fletcher wasn't my father?" Bryce said blankly.

"Nossir. Your mom told me about Neil one time when I was on the night shift and she couldn't sleep. She loved her husband and he was good to her. A good man. That's what she said. *He was a good man.* Lots worse things can go on a headstone than that."

His brain reeling, Bryce said, "I always called Fletcher *Dad*. He never contradicted me. Nor did my mother."

"He didn't like the thought of some other man fathering her kid. He was a mean sonofabitch, if you'll pardon me for saying so." Maybelline daintily flicked a cookie crumb onto the floor.

"You're not telling me anything I don't already know. Was that why he used to belt my mom? Jealousy?"

"Jealousy, drink, natural cussedness. Some men just can't keep their fists to themselves, and he was one of 'em."

"Why did she stay with him?"

"She didn't have two cents to rub together, no schooling to speak of though she was bright enough, and she was pregnant when she met him. He was good-looking, I s'pose, and when he chose to he could charm canaries from a pear tree. And she had you to look after, don't forget. She told me that's when she ran away to the shelter, the day he hit you so hard you flew clean 'cross the room. That was when she said *enough*...she loved you like the sun rose and set on you, though she might never have said so. Not a woman to say two words if one would do."

Bryce's heart was thumping as though once again he was that little boy wielding a rusty truck at Fletcher Laribee. "Why did she leave me at the shelter if she loved me so much?" he said, and heard the sharp edges of that old pain in his voice.

"That's the part I'm real surprised you don't know about. Can't figure out how come they never told you." Maybelline gave a heavy sigh. "So I guess it's up to me. We'll never know for sure what happened...I can only tell you what I believe. You can see by the posters on the wall that I like the soaps. But what happened back then wasn't no soap. It was for real. And there wasn't a happy ending, neither."

Her face sagged; for the first time she wouldn't meet

Bryce's eyes. "The night she disappeared, Rose told me she was going back to your apartment to get some of her stuff. A couple of photos, the old ring she had from her mother, that kind of thing. I told her not to be so foolish. Or else to take someone with her. But no, she was set on going by herself and getting back all the faster. She had plans, you see. For you and her. Plans to get on the bus and start out afresh somewhere else where no one knew her, and Fletcher wouldn't find her."

Bryce wrapped his cold fingers around his cup. "Why didn't she come back?"

Gazing down at the floor, Maybelline said, "They found her the next day. At the bottom of the stairs with her neck broke."

Bryce paled. "Dead. She was dead...that's why she left me at the shelter." Briefly he covered his face with his hands.

"That's right, she was dead. I'm real sorry to be the one to tell you."

"I always wondered why she didn't come back for me," Bryce said in a muffled voice.

"Ordinarily, nothing would've stopped her," Maybelline said. "There was no sign of Fletcher that day, nor ever after that I heard. They held one of them inquests and called it death by misadventure, which is a downright stupid word when you come to think about it."

Bryce looked up, aghast. "You think he did it. Fletcher."

"That's what my bones tell me happened that evening. But I can never prove it. Maybe she slipped and fell. Or maybe she was pushed."

"Either way, she was dead," he said bitterly.

"They took you away before my next shift, to a care home way 'cross the city. By the time I got there, you were in a foster home and they wouldn't tell me where. They never would give out that kind of information.

Against city policy, or some such fancy words—that's what they said.''

Bryce rested his hand on her wrinkled fingers. "It was good of you to go looking for me."

Maybelline wiped a tear from the corner of her eye with her apron. "I just don't understand why they never told you your mom was dead. Maybe not right away...I can see that, you were just little. But you should've been told later on."

"I moved around a lot," Bryce said dryly. "I wasn't what you'd call a model kid. So I never stopped in one place very long."

"That's no excuse. It's downright disgraceful, keeping you in the dark all those years." She scowled. "I bet they'd have some more of their fancy words to cover it up. Failure in communication. Mislaid records. When what they really mean is that they done wrong."

The old woman looked very fierce. Bryce said, "I always assumed she'd upped and left me. That I was too much trouble for her and for Fletcher."

"For Fletcher, yeah. But for Rose? No way. I liked Rose, liked her a lot. She was doing her best, which is all any of us can do. I was saddened that she died like that. Still am."

"I'll find out where she's buried. Would you go with me one day and we'll leave some roses on her grave?"

"She's in the old cemetery five blocks east of here. And I'd be right pleased to do that with you."

"So you even found out where she was buried."

"Least I could do."

"If my dad—my real dad—was a good man, you're a saint, Maybelline Parker."

"Get away with you," she said and poured him more tea.

A couple of hours later, Bryce was striding down the street through the heat of early evening. He walked for a long time, his shoulders hunched, his eyes trained on the sidewalk; and something in his face kept anyone from accosting him. It was only when he realized that his feet had carried him back to his car that he knew what he had to do. Climbing in, he headed out of the city. West, toward Wellspring.

It was already dark. He had no real idea where the time had gone, only that each and every footstep he'd taken had pounded a single word into his ears. Murder.

Murder or accident, his mother had fully intended to stay with her four-year-old son, and build a better life for him. But because of bureaucratic bungling, that information had been denied him all these years.

It started to rain before he hit the highway, hard drops that splattered against the windshield. He slowed down, in no hurry to get to Jenessa's because he didn't really know why he was going. Only that he had no choice.

When he drove down the little lane, his tires splashing through the puddles, the Quaker cottage was in total darkness. It was just past eleven. Jenessa had gone to bed.

Bryce leaned back against the leather seat. His shoulders felt like he'd been lifting weights for two hours straight, while his head was pounding from a combination of caffeine and emotion. He was, he knew, too tired to turn right around and drive back to Boston.

He'd catnap for a few minutes. Then he'd go back.

There was no point in disturbing her. What was he going to say? If he'd only stopped to think before driving all this way, he could have saved himself the journey.

The metallic snap of raindrops on the roof was oddly soothing. Within moments Bryce was fast asleep.

Jenessa woke to the rumble and snarl of thunder.

She liked storms. She lay still, waiting until lightning's brief brilliance lit up the room before getting out of bed and padding into the kitchen to get a drink of water. The thunder was getting closer all the time. The garden needed the rain, she thought, and went to check that the front windows were closed.

A car was parked in the lane. A Jaguar just like Bryce's.

As the next bolt of electricity lit up the sky, she saw a figure slumped in the front seat.

With a gasp of fear she grabbed a flashlight from the shelf in the mudroom, thrust her feet into her rubber boots and threw on her rain slicker. Why was Bryce here in the middle of the night? Was he ill? Had something happened to Travis?

As she left the shelter of the back porch, the rain dashed against her face, almost blinding her. Her slicker blew in the wind like a witch's cape. Slithering in the mud, Jenessa turned onto the lane and reached his car. Raising her fist, she banged on the window and yelled his name.

In the yellow shaft of light she saw Bryce start, his eyes flying open. For a moment she was certain he had no idea where he was, and again she shouted his name.

This time he stared full into the beam of her flashlight. He looked terrible, she thought, and braced herself for bad news. Then he took the keys out of the ignition, reached for the door handle and hauled himself out of the car.

"Come into the house," she begged, "hurry."

Leading the way as another lightning bolt bathed the garden in an eerie shade of blue, Jenessa ran for the back door. She held it open for him, and as quickly closed it behind him. Switching off her flashlight, she said shakily, "You're soaked."

"Yeah…I meant to drive back, and I must have fallen asleep."

There were bruised shadows under his eyes. "What's wrong, Bryce?" she asked, holding her voice steady with an effort. "Why did you drive out here so late?"

"I found out about my parents," he said.

"Your parents?" Jenessa faltered. "Then nothing's wrong with Travis? Or Julie and the baby?"

He frowned, raking his fingers through his wet hair.

"What do you mean? I haven't talked to them in over a week."

"It doesn't matter," she said rapidly. "Here, sit down and I'll get you an old shirt of Travis's—he gave it to me for gardening and it'll fit you just fine."

In a moment she was back. Bryce was still sitting where she'd left him, his gray eyes opaque. She knelt to undo the buttons of his shirt, and pulled on the dry one; then, because he was shivering, she wrapped a throw over his shoulders and put the kettle on.

It was this that roused him. "Don't make tea," he muttered. "I drank some today that was strong enough to walk on. Maybe that's why I kept having nightmares."

"Have you eaten?"

He said vaguely, "I guess not. Not since noon."

Five minutes later, Jenessa put a steaming bowl of homemade soup in front of him, with some of Wilma Lawson's crusty bread. "Eat," she said. "Then we'll talk."

He devoured the food like a man who was starving. Then he pushed back the bowl. "My real father died before I was born, leaving my mother a widow," he said tonelessly. "Fletcher was my stepfather, not my biological father."

As Jenessa gave a startled gasp, Bryce went on, "The reason my mother didn't come back to the shelter to get me was because she was dead. Found with her neck broken at the bottom of a flight of stairs. Fletcher might or might not have pushed her. I'll never know. Not unless I track him down and beat the truth out of him."

"So she didn't abandon you," Jenessa whispered.

"No. She was planning on the two of us taking off, and starting over." His voice cracked. "But she never got the chance. And all these years nobody thought to tell me she was dead."

He dropped his head into his hands; a long shudder ran through his body. Swiftly Jenessa wrapped her arms around him, holding him close. Then she whispered, "Did you find anything out about your real father?"

"His name was Neil Jackson. His middle name was Bryce. He was a good man, according to my mother. Had he lived, I suppose he'd have given me a decent, normal childhood. Like any kid deserves."

"So much waste," Jenessa said, appalled.

"Yeah…I came here to tell you about it, but you'd gone to bed. I was planning to drive back but I must have gone out like a light."

"I'm glad you're here," she said simply. "If you've had enough to eat, let's go to bed, Bryce."

It was a measure of the shock he'd sustained that Bryce got into bed beside her without any argument. As she held him close, he fell asleep with the suddenness of the little boy he'd been; with his eyes closed, his face had the vulnerability of that little boy.

Lightning flickered through the curtains. Thunder growled like a caged wolf. Against her cheek Jenessa could feel the warmth of Bryce's breathing, infinitely precious to her. *I'm in love with you,* she thought. *I've fallen head over heels in love with you and I never realized it until now.*

Her palm was curved around his rib cage, her thighs tucked into his. Of course she was in love with him. As a gust of rain hammered the windowpane, her eyes widened in the dark. She'd probably been in love with him ever since she was seventeen. One more reason why she'd never ventured into another man's bed.

Complex, passionate Bryce, the man who brought her body to fulfillment and enlivened her soul. As happiness flooded her in an irresistible tide, she hugged it to her much as she was holding his sleeping body.

She'd been mistaken to worry that she was unable to love anyone. Her mother, her father…and now Bryce: her heart had expanded to include them all.

How lucky she was.

Jenessa was drifting off to sleep herself when a very obvious thought jerked her eyes open. Bryce no longer had to fear that he carried in his blood Fletcher Laribee's violence. Fletcher was only his stepfather, not his true father. Furthermore, Rose, his mother, hadn't abandoned and betrayed him; she'd died instead. Did that mean that maybe, just maybe, Bryce would rethink the whole question of commitment? Would he understand that he could allow himself more than a temporary liaison?

Would he fall in love with her?

CHAPTER FOURTEEN

IT WAS midmorning before Jenessa woke. Bathed in a warm sensuality, she realized a man's body was pressed to hers, a body all too ready to make love to her. She smiled at Bryce. "Yes, please," she said.

Laughter banished the shadows from his face. "You're easy."

"Where you're concerned."

She might lack the courage to tell him she loved him in so many words; but she could show him with her body, she thought, and nibbled at his lips with exquisite sensuality. "What a lovely surprise to find you in my bed—it's a great way to wake up."

"I'm not inclined to argue," he said with a lazy grin. But his eyes were sparked with fire and his arm pulled her strongly into his body, so warm, so well known, so infinitely desirable.

Catching fire from him, she kissed him with all the eroticism he aroused in her. With a suddenness that inflamed her, he pushed her thighs open and thrust between them. More than ready for him, Jenessa matched her rhythms to his, achingly aware of his hands on her breasts, her waist and hips. She writhed beneath him until the world exploded into light and color and there was nothing left but the rapid pounding of his heart and her own blood racing through her veins.

Bryce buried his face in her hair. "Sorry," he gasped, "that was way too fast."

"You don't hear me complaining."

"I—I just had to know that you were there. Real. Not a dream. I know I'm not making any sense."

156

She said, allowing her newly discovered love to soften her voice, "Bryce, I'm here for you. For as long as you want."

"You're more than I deserve," he said roughly.

She had no idea how to reply to this. "Anyway," she said pertly, "we've got all morning. Or at least, I have."

He nuzzled her shoulder with his lips. "You figure I'm leaving for Boston right now?"

"Maybe not right now...oh, do that again."

Obligingly he did so; as he did, the telephone shrilled from the kitchen. Jenessa said faintly, "Whoever wants me to pick that up is out of luck. Bryce, you're driving me crazy, I can't get enough of you..." Then, for quite some time, she stopped talking altogether.

The phone rang again, early in the afternoon. But Jenessa had informed Bryce half an hour earlier that it was her turn to seduce him: with enthusiasm and a charming assertiveness she brought to play all her newly discovered skills, along with the sure knowledge of what drove him to the brink. Afterward, they both fell sound asleep.

It was past three when Jenessa woke to find Bryce leaning on one elbow, watching her. She smiled at him drowsily. "Where's my lunch? Caviar and champagne'll do."

"How about bread and cheese?"

"That'll do, too...I'm starving."

"Beat you to the shower."

Predictably this further delayed lunch. Jenessa was slicing bread, an idiotic grin on her face, and Bryce was rummaging in the refrigerator when a knock came at the front door. Puzzled, Jenessa said, "Who could that be?"

Trying to comb a little order into her hair with her fingers, she headed for the door and pulled it open. "Hi, sis," Travis said.

"Oh," said Jenessa. "Hi. Julie...and Samantha. Come in." She blushed. "Bryce is here, we were just making lunch."

Travis eyed her scarlet cheeks. "Lunch? Kind of late in the day for that."

Bryce came out from the kitchen, a bunch of lettuce in one hand and a hunk of cheese in the other. "Want a sandwich?" he said. "What are you doing down this way?"

"We're on our way to a medical conference in New York. Decided to take our time and drive. Didn't you get our message?"

"Message?" Jenessa repeated, wishing her intelligence would catch up with her blush reflex.

"We phoned," Travis explained patiently. "A couple of times."

Bryce grinned, making no attempt to sound convincing. "We must have been out in the garden."

"Anyway, do come in," Jenessa said, flustered. "Do you want to put Samantha in the bedroom, Julie?" She had, thank heavens, made the bed. "And I've just made iced tea."

"She should sleep for another hour or two," Julie said; she was wearing a tailored sundress, her sleek hair gleaming. "You look great, Jenessa."

"Thanks," said Jenessa and blushed again.

Travis said blandly, "Glad to see you're taking some time off, Bryce. You work too hard."

Jenessa fled to the bedroom. Bryce's socks were on the chair. As she picked them up, wondering which drawer she should hide them in, Julie said kindly, "We didn't mean to take you by surprise. But Travis always likes taking the back roads, and we figured if you were home, it would be nice to drop in. And I do know about the birds and the bees, Jenessa."

Jenessa turned around, the socks clutched in her hand. "I'm still learning," she muttered.

"I'm sure you've got the best of teachers."

"Julie, I—this is only temporary. Bryce and me."

Julie rested her hand on Jenessa's bare arm. "How do

you know, so soon?'' she said. ''Bryce had a tough life when he was a boy, that's bound to mark him.''

Sudden tears flooded Jenessa's eyes. ''I wish you weren't going to Mexico...just when you and I are starting to get to know each other.''

''We'll be back. And you must come for a visit. You could bring Bryce if you want to.''

Carefully she tilted Samantha's car seat backward against the pillows. Jenessa turned away from the baby's sleeping face, so trusting and vulnerable. Bryce must have been like that, once. But by the age of four he'd been exposed to more than any child should know.

She blinked hard and walked back into the kitchen, her back very straight. Bryce and Travis were making sandwiches together: the two men she loved most in the world.

Smarten up, Jenessa. You want the whole world to know you're head over heels in love with your brother's best friend?

She said brightly, ''I'll get a couple of tomatoes from the garden.''

When she came back in, the red globes in her hand still warm from the afternoon sun, Travis said easily, ''Any new paintings, Jen?''

''One,'' she said. ''It's for Dad.'' And quickly she filled in the details of her visit with Charles the week before.

Travis said quietly, ''Good for you.''

Those three small words felt like an accolade. Shyly Jenessa led the way into the studio, where her latest painting stood on the easel. With meticulous realism she'd depicted a hedge of purple lilacs against a stone wall; to one side, wraithlike in the dusk, a little girl was dancing on the grass. Bryce said abruptly, ''That's you.''

She nodded. Travis added, ''I can almost smell the lilacs.''

''I hope Dad will like it,'' Jenessa said.

''It's lovely,'' Julie said, ''I'm sure he will.''

Jenessa knew the painting wasn't the breakthrough she

was waiting for; she also knew that working on it had given her great pleasure. And with that, she was content.

As they sat around the kitchen table, Travis said, "We're hoping you two will do us a favor. I'd like to take Julie to dinner at the inn in Masefield. Would you baby-sit for us?"

"Look after Samantha? On my own?" Jenessa squeaked. "What if she cried?"

"Pick her up. Besides, Bryce'll keep you company," Travis said. "We'll come and get her after we eat—we're booked into the local B and B overnight. Come on, sis...Julie and I need a candlelit dinner for two."

"Red wine and death-by-chocolate," Julie said dreamily.

"Holding hands under the table," her husband grinned. "Diapers and romance don't always go together. And the two of you are Samantha's godparents, it's time you lived up to some of those vows you made."

Bryce laughed. "Laying on a guilt trip, Travis? Cheer up, Jenessa, it can't be that difficult to look after a baby. You put food in one end, and you clean up the other."

"Will you hang around?" she said suspiciously. "Since you're such an expert."

"Yes, ma'am...you afraid of twelve pounds of baby?"

"Of course not," she said, not altogether truthfully. What was she afraid of? Looking after her niece in the company of her lover?

She found out shortly after Travis and Julie had left, when Samantha did wake up crying. "I was hoping she'd sleep all evening," Jenessa said. "Why don't you get her, Bryce?"

"You're a woman—you're supposed to know about babies."

"I stayed with a friend's baby once when I was young, and he screamed for four hours straight. I changed him, fed him, rocked him, sang to him—you name it, I did it. I've never looked after a baby since."

"The one and only time I've ever held a baby was at the christening. You may have noticed she screamed blue murder the whole time."

"You're a man—you're supposed to stand fast in the face of danger."

Bryce grinned at her. "Why don't we both get Samantha? Strength in numbers and all that."

"It's a plan."

In the bedroom Jenessa awkwardly gathered the baby into her arms; Samantha's little face was screwed up like a monkey's and she was bellowing at the top of her lungs. Bryce warmed a bottle on the stove while Jenessa fumbled with diaper tabs and soapy water; as though sensing Jenessa's inexperience, Samantha cried all the harder. Bryce passed Jenessa the bottle. The baby latched onto it as though she hadn't eaten in days; a few minutes later, when Jenessa patted her on the back, she was rewarded by a juicy belch and a wet-cheeked smile. "Hey," said Bryce, "you've got the hang of it."

Jenessa gaped at him as one by one the words tumbled through her mind. *So that's what I want,* she thought in utter clarity. *Marriage, children, love and commitment...all with Bryce. No one else will do. And nothing less.*

She thrust the child at him. "You feed her the rest. I'll clean up the table."

But Bryce was staring at her, and made no move to take Samantha. "What's going on, Jenessa?"

"Nothing! What do you mean?" she gabbled. "We're both godparents—it's your turn to do some of the work."

Bryce said harshly, "I never fed a baby in my life."

"She won't care."

Samantha gave a fretful whimper. And Bryce, feeling as though he was crossing his own personal Rubicon, lifted the baby from Jenessa's arms.

When he'd held Samantha at the christening, all he'd been aware of was how hard she was crying. But now, through her cotton nightgown, he allowed himself to feel the warmth of her little body; she was gazing at him unblinkingly with her big blue eyes. He gazed back, a lump in his throat, as she produced a charming, toothless grin. Hastily he jammed the teat in her mouth. She started to suck lustily.

Feeling inordinately proud of himself, as though he'd achieved something quite remarkable, Bryce said, "This isn't so difficult." When Samantha had drained the bottle, he dandled her in his lap. She was so small, so helpless.

How could anyone hurt a child?

The question had come into his head without conscious volition; but once there, he couldn't dislodge it. He'd done his best to keep his mother's fate at bay ever since he'd left Maybelline's yesterday evening. But it was there nevertheless, dark and heavy, ultimately unknowable. Had his mother felt this same flood of tenderness when she'd held him in her arms?

He'd never know the answer to that question.

"Bryce," Jenessa whispered, "what's wrong?"

He looked at the woman standing by the stove, the overhead light glinting in the wild mass of her hair. What if this was his baby, his and Jenessa's? How would he feel then? Would he protect his child from harm, as a father should? Or would he hurt it, as Fletcher had?

More questions he couldn't answer, he thought grimly. The kind of questions that made him want to run for his life.

"We should put her back to bed," he said, distantly pleased with how normal he sounded.

"Yes," she said steadily, "and then you can tell me what's going on."

Maybe I will, he thought, going back into the bedroom. And maybe I won't. How could he, even to himself, have admitted the possibility of having a child with Jenessa? In his books, children meant commitment. Meant love.

He didn't love Jenessa.

But did she love him? After tucking Samantha into her little bed, he stood still, frowning at the wall. All along, Jenessa had denied having such feelings for him. But was she telling the truth?

He remembered the radiance in her face when they'd made love this morning, the tenderness that had imbued all her movements. What were they, if not love?

What had she said to him? *I'm here for you. For as long as you want.* Weren't they the words of a woman in love?

He didn't want Jenessa falling in love with him, he couldn't handle it. It was that simple.

Samantha, slurping at her fist, had settled down immediately. So Bryce had no excuse to linger in the bedroom. And he couldn't very well leave for Boston now, Travis wouldn't be impressed. So he walked back into the kitchen, where Jenessa was making tea, and said easily, "We're a couple of pros when it comes to babies."

"Bryce," she said, clutching the teapot to her chest, "you told me the bare bones of your parents' story last night. But not how you felt about any of it."

"It's too soon to know."

"You must have some feelings!"

"Don't push me, Jenessa," he said tautly.

"How else am I to find out what's going on inside you?"

"Why do you need to?"

She flinched. "We slept together last night. Then we made love most of the day. Doesn't that mean anything to you?"

"Of course it does! But it's got nothing to do with my parents."

"What does it mean to you, Bryce?"

Her chin was raised. But beneath the defiance in her blue eyes, fear lurked. She was afraid of the answer, he realized, afraid of what he might—or might not—say. His suspicion that she had indeed fallen in love with him deepened to something very near conviction. He tamped down a rising anger and in a hard voice repeated, "Just don't push me, okay?"

With a superhuman effort, she swallowed the retort that was hovering on her tongue. "Okay," she said. "I can't be pushed into painting something I'm not ready to paint...the same would apply to you, I suppose, about your parents."

Bryce hadn't expected such understanding. He said roughly, "You're a remarkable woman."

Her eyes suddenly swam with unshed tears. "I'm a pushy and opinionated artist who hasn't got a clue what she's going to paint next...nothing very remarkable about that."

"You're honest and you listen, and if Travis and Julie weren't about to walk in the door, and if there wasn't a baby in the middle of the bed, guess where I'd be taking you?"

So, for now, their affair had as its boundaries the bedroom, Jenessa thought. That was what he meant. But for how long could she accept such boundaries? She said lightly, "I'm going to try and catch up with that pile of newspapers on the coffee table." Sitting down on the couch, she picked up the top one and buried her face in it.

As it happened, Travis and Julie didn't arrive for another hour. They walked up the path hand in hand, and once in the house they didn't linger; Bryce didn't have to be a genius to see that Travis had passion on his mind. He called after them, "Hope Samantha stays asleep," and was rewarded with a grin from his old friend.

Then he turned to Jenessa, swung her up into his arms, carried her into the bedroom and made love to her in utter silence and with a kind of desperation. Afterward, his heart still pounding in his chest, he said, "I'm going back to Boston now, Jenessa—I've got appointments all day tomorrow, then I'm meeting with the architect at five—

he said he'd have some blueprints ready. But I'll call you before the weekend.''

In the semidarkness his eyes were like black pits; and their tumultuous lovemaking had, for the first time, left Jenessa unsatisfied. Not physically, that was impossible. But her heart felt empty and cold. She was also very frightened. Doing her best to mask this fear, which was as strong as it was irrational, she said evenly, "Do I have any say in that decision?''

"I'm doing the best I can—that's all I can tell you,'' Bryce said in a raw voice; and with that she had to be satisfied. She stood by the front window, watching his taillights disappear into the night, aware of a crushing loneliness. How could she be lonely when she'd just spent the better part of twenty-four hours with Bryce?

If he wouldn't share his joys and sorrows with her, his fears and dreams, then she was lost. Loving him as she did, how could she be satisfied with less than all of him?

Loving him as she did...perhaps, she thought, standing still in the middle of the kitchen, trust was an integral part of love. She simply had to trust that Bryce would, sooner or later, open his soul to her.

What other option did she have?

The scent of his body was imprinted on her skin; just to recall his touch, the huskiness in his voice, his face convulsed at climax, made Jenessa long for him all over again. She prowled around the kitchen, washing a few dishes, tidying, her mind far from what she was doing. Then she walked into the studio, picked up her sketch pad and let the charcoal cover page after page. It was well after midnight when she went to bed.

She woke at first light. Chewing on a banana, she went into the studio and stationed herself in front of a blank canvas. She stared at it for a long time before she picked up the first tube of paint and squeezed some onto her palette. And even then, she waited to pick up her brush.

Utterly absorbed, occasionally stopping to stretch her

legs or her back and wander around the house, Jenessa worked the whole day; and had she been asked, couldn't have described the emotions and ideas that she was painting. When the light began to fade, she made a few last adjustments; and then stood back.

It was finished. It was, she thought slowly, the most significant painting she'd ever done; it was unquestionably a complete break from her previous work. Abstract, yet with recognizable elements, full of color and infused with joy: there wasn't a trace of the menace that had haunted her work for months...exhaustion washed over her in a great wave. She cleaned her brushes, made sure all her paints were capped, and fell into bed. Within moments she was deeply and dreamlessly asleep.

CHAPTER FIFTEEN

BRYCE pushed open the screen door. He'd knocked twice, with no result. Neither the screen nor the front door was locked. Sure, Jenessa lived in the country and knew all her neighbors; but she should be more careful, particularly now that the sun had set, darkness hovering in the corners of the porch. He stepped inside.

The house was bathed in shadows and silence. There were dirty dishes on the counter, dishes left from yesterday, he realized. He should have checked the garden first, she might be lingering outside where it was cooler.

To go out the back, he had to walk past Jenessa's bedroom. The door was ajar. She was sprawled, facedown, on the covers, wearing paint-streaked trousers and an old shirt; she was sound asleep, her breathing even and quiet. The soles of her bare feet filled him with any number of emotions that he didn't want to label. Instinctively he headed for the studio and switched on the light.

The wide pine floorboards creaked underfoot. The single painting on the easel caught him by the throat. Beauty was an overused word, so Bryce had sometimes thought; but, without a doubt, the wild mélange of color and motion in front of him was beautiful. He stood still, letting it speak to him, allowing its joy to penetrate his pores, a joy that was almost sacred in its intensity.

Then, very slowly, the joy subsided, to be replaced by a deep unease. He'd been right, he thought. All those little signals he'd been picking up had been dead on target. Although until now, Jenessa's paintings had lacked something, but this one was complete. She wasn't stuck any more. It was all very obvious: Jenessa had fallen in love

167

with him. And, in her usual fashion, she'd used the medium of paint and canvas to pour out her feelings in a way that was tangible.

Dimly, from behind him, he heard the pad of her feet crossing the old floorboards. He turned to face her; it wasn't until he spoke that he realized the depth of his feelings. "You're in love with me," he accused.

She stopped in her tracks, pushing her hair back from her face. "Yes," she said, "I am."

For once, her honesty appalled him. "From the beginning, I warned you against that."

"You did, yes."

"I told you this was an affair! That I wasn't into commitment or marriage."

Her eyes narrowed. "Why are you so angry?"

His breath hissed between his teeth. "Because you've known this for some time and haven't said anything."

"Only since I brought you in out of the rain and we fell asleep in each other's arms."

"Since I told you about my parents—so you feel sorry for me."

"The one thing I do not feel is sorry for you! And kindly explain why I'm supposed to tell you I've been stupid enough to fall in love with you when you won't even tell me how you feel about your father and mother?"

He said savagely, "Everything's happened too fast. You and me. This affair. I don't know what the hell I'm doing in bed or out. With you or without you."

"You won't allow yourself to know."

Her logic infuriated him. "I need time away from you, Jenessa."

"You're ending our affair?" she said in a strained voice. "I don't know why I'm surprised—I always knew you would."

"I'm not ending it! But I've got to get away for a while. I need a break. Breathing space."

"So that's what you came to tell me?" she flashed. "All the way from Boston?"

Why had he come? Because he'd worked all day, and he'd needed to meander the peace of her garden? Because the architect's plans had excited him and he'd wanted to tell her about them?

Or was it because the only man he felt sure of right now was the man he became in her bed?

He said flatly, "Do I have to have an explanation for everything? The city was stifling, and I'd had enough of it. What more do you want?"

Her face very pale, she took a step backward. "I want a man with the courage to share more than his body."

"Then let me tell you what I did after my meetings this morning," he grated. "I looked up back issues of the newspaper for the dates around my mother's death. She warranted one small paragraph the day after she died—it said she'd been found with a broken neck at the foot of the stairs, and that the police were looking for Fletcher Laribee to help with their enquiries. No further mention after that. Not one word. She was dirt poor. Expendable. No one wanted to read about her life or her death."

"Maybelline did."

"Then she was the only one. Unless you count Fletcher. So then I went to the police, asked to see the file. Fletcher was never located, and the case is considered closed for lack of evidence."

"You could hire someone to track him down."

"That won't bring my mother back."

Jenessa spoke the obvious. "So you're convinced Fletcher pushed her down the stairs?"

"You're damn right I am. My mother was light on her feet, nimble. Sometimes, when Fletcher was gone for the day, she'd turn on the radio and dance around the room—I remember her doing that once, she was wearing a blue skirt and her hair was tied back with a ribbon."

"That's a lovely memory," Jenessa said softly.

His face hardened. "She'd learned how to dodge him, to stay out of the way of his fists. She's the last person who'd fall down a flight of stairs. You asked yesterday how I felt about my parents. How do you think I feel, knowing that my stepfather killed my mother and got away with it?"

"It's tragic, Bryce—truly tragic," she whispered. "But at least you know Fletcher wasn't your real father."

"He's the only father I ever knew. He's the one who shaped me."

"I don't believe that!"

Bryce suddenly stepped closer to her, wrapping his fingers around her arms with bruising strength. "What if you screamed now, Jenessa? Would your neighbors hear? Or are you too far away from the nearest house?"

"Stop it!" she cried. "I've never once been physically afraid of you, I told you that before...you'd never strike me or push me around, you're not that kind of man."

"How do you know?" he asked very softly. "How well can you ever know another person?"

She loosened his fingers with her own, pulling free. "Are you trying to frighten me so I'll send you away? So you can keep a safe distance from intimacy, and you won't ever have to confront your feelings?"

"I'm warning you against easy sentimentality, that's what I'm doing. Love—it's the most abused word in the language."

"Don't you dare cheapen my feelings! Or belittle them. I'm twenty-nine years old and you're the first man I've ever fallen in love with. There's nothing remotely cute or sentimental about the love I feel for you. It's elemental. And utterly real."

"Then you picked the wrong man," Bryce said.

Jenessa took another step away from him, rubbing her arms where he'd gripped her; but even then she didn't give up. "Do you want to be alone for the rest of your life, Bryce—unmarried, no children, no one to love you?

Do you think that's what your mother would want as her legacy?''

''You leave my mother out of this.''

''How can I? She was a woman who could still dance, even though she was in that awful situation. She had more guts than her son!''

Fury surged through his body. ''I'm not staying here to listen to this,'' he said with lethal softness.

''She didn't abandon you, Bryce—she loved you.''

''I know that now,'' he rasped. ''But for thirty-two years I didn't.''

Jenessa said steadily, ''You've never told me where you lived from the time you were four until you went to Travis's school.''

''Foster home number one. They fed me pop and chips and pocketed the care money. That fell apart when I started school and arrived hungry every day. In foster home number two, I was bullied for a solid year by three of the older boys in the house. So I ran away. They put me in a group home. I ran away. At ten I was caught stealing and sent to reform school. I ran away. Then, finally, someone got the message and put me in a half-decent place; although by then, of course, I wasn't about to let my guard down. But I did go back to school on a regular basis, and the rest you know—computers, a scholarship, and Travis.''

''When you said Travis saved your life, you meant it,'' Jenessa faltered.

There were tears in her eyes. Bryce didn't want to see them. ''Quit feeling sorry for me.''

''Quit simplifying all my emotions!''

Aware of a flash of admiration for her stubbornness, Bryce said, ''I'm backing off, Jenessa. I've got to get away from you for a while and figure out what's going on.''

''Why not figure it out with me?''

"Because you're in love with me," he said with brutal honesty.

"So it's all my fault."

"I warned you not to fall in love. In no way did I deceive you."

"I'm caught, aren't I?" Her shoulders drooped. "If I say I won't wait for you, then I'm proving what you already believe—that love isn't to be trusted, it's not steadfast. But if I do wait for you, then I'm doing just that—waiting. My life on hold until you decide that running away is the same thing as being stuck."

She was using his own words against him. Bryce said furiously, "I wish to God I'd never seen that painting."

Jenessa folded her arms across her chest. "You can't hide from the truth forever."

"From your version of it," he snarled. While he was driving out here, he'd pictured a calm, rational discussion in which he'd explain why he needed to retreat for a while. If he'd imagined Jenessa's reaction at all, he'd seen her peacefully agreeing that his course of action was indeed the best one for both of them. The reality had been excruciatingly different. He was angrier with Jenessa than he'd been with anyone for a very long time. Simultaneously, of course, and making nonsense of everything he'd said, he wanted to take her to bed. Right now.

Sure, Bryce. She'd scratch your eyes out if you tried.

"I'm not ending our relationship," he repeated in a voice from which he did his level best to remove any emotion. "I go to Paris and Hamburg next week. But I'll be in touch on the weekend when I get back."

This was Thursday. So for nine days she wouldn't know her own fate; worse, she'd begin to understand the cost of waiting.

Jenessa tossed her head. "I'm not going to sit by the phone all weekend, if that's what you expect."

The words dragged out of him, Bryce said, "Take care of yourself."

"I've managed to do that for twenty-nine years without you. I'm sure I can manage another week and a half."

"You're determined to have the last word!"

"It's all I'm getting, isn't it, Bryce?" she said in a low voice. "But I don't want the last word. I want you."

It took every ounce of Bryce's willpower not to take her in his arms and kiss her with all the passion of which he was capable. Passion that she herself had unleashed. Knowing that if he touched her, he'd be lost, he said tightly, "I'll talk to you when I get back. 'Bye, Jenessa."

Then he wheeled and headed out the door. After taking the front steps two at a time, he ran toward his car

Who was he running away from? Jenessa? Or himself?

Left alone, Jenessa clenched her nails into her palms so hard that it hurt. She wouldn't cry. She wouldn't.

How dare Bryce imply she had an adolescent crush on him? That her love was nothing but cheap sentimentality? How dare he turn his back on her, even though she'd fought for him with every weapon at her command?

Except her body. She'd disdained to use that.

But nothing she'd said had made any impression on him. He was locked in the past, determined to run his life by those old scripts. She couldn't change that. Only he could.

And he wasn't willing.

For all his denials, was he, deep down, intent on abandoning her?

She grabbed an apple from the fruit bowl and dug her teeth into it. Hungry? How could she be anything so mundane as hungry when her heart was breaking? When she was so angry she could throw the apple clear across the room? All her movements jerky and uncoordinated, Jenessa made some toast and ate it with a chunk of cheese and the apple. Then she stalked into the studio. The painting that had caused all the trouble was the first thing she saw; cursing it under her breath, she stacked it unceremoniously on the floor against some other canvasses and picked up her sketch pad.

She had to do something with the turmoil in her breast. Because below the anger, she knew, lay hurt, a hurt deeper than words. Bryce had left her. Temporarily, so he'd said. But then everything about this love affair was temporary.

She was beginning to hate the sound of the word.

Would he be back? Or would he take this opportunity to end their affair? Clamping down on terror, she began to draw; then she made a preliminary oil on a small board. Drained, she turned out the light, fighting back tears.

She had to get some sleep.

She did sleep fitfully, waking at dawn from a nightmare where she was being bullied in a group home that was stashed wall-high with computers. After forcing herself to eat some breakfast, Jenessa went back into the studio.

She worked like a woman possessed for nearly five hours, until intuition warned her that she'd done all she could. Standing back, she gazed at what she'd produced.

The whole painting spoke of the temporary. Love, happiness, life itself, were all transitory and soon to be lost.

Her back aching, Jenessa cleaned her brushes. Then, moving like a much older woman, she walked stiffly into her bedroom and lay facedown on the bed. Clutching the corners of the pillow in her clenched fists, she felt sobs crowd her throat, forcing their way upward. She wept for a long time, out of a loneliness blacker than any she'd ever known.

Bryce had shown her the miracle of intimacy; and now had snatched it away. How could she not be lonely?

Why had she been so stupid, so unutterably foolish, as to fall in love with him?

CHAPTER SIXTEEN

A BACK STREET in the Left Bank district of Paris, well past midnight. Once again, Bryce couldn't settle down to sleep in his luxurious hotel room; once again, he'd taken to the streets in an effort to tire himself out.

Hamburg had been the same. Business had gone well in both Germany and France; he was far too professional to allow his inner confusion to show, let alone get in the way of the expertise and creative thinking that were his trademark. But when he wasn't working, he was a walking disaster.

Literally, he thought wryly, striding along the worn cobblestones, catching a glimpse of the river between two buildings. He'd got up at dawn and jogged for an hour, and at noon had availed himself of the company fitness center with its weights and rowing machines; yet here he was, as restless as the wind-rippled Seine.

He still had no idea what he was going to say to Jenessa when he phoned her. That he missed her day and night, her absence as pervasive as a missing limb? That the intensity of feelings she aroused in him terrified him? That his past enclosed him as claustrophobically as the dark alleys he was passing?

She was no slouch. He wouldn't be telling her anything she didn't already know.

He couldn't keep her waiting forever; that wouldn't be fair. The next step was up to him. Underlying his confusion was the sure knowledge that the decision he made this weekend would affect the rest of his life. A watershed.

The breeze ruffled his hair. He increased his pace, came

175

around a corner and briefly saw the tableau in front of him as though it was frozen in time. Two men, balaclavas pulled over their faces, and a cowering woman.

Bryce ran straight for them, his brain working at top speed. He'd learned any number of dirty moves on the back streets of Boston; and had added to that in his twenties a brown belt in karate. As one of the men snatched at the woman's purse and the other raised his fists to knock her down, Bryce gave a ferocious yell, tripped the first man so he fell with a bruising thud onto the stones, and swung the other man around to meet his own fists. From the corner of his eye he saw the fallen attacker stagger to his feet. Whirling, he flattened him with a single kick. The second man turned to flee, abandoning the purse and his accomplice; who, groaning, dragged himself out of Bryce's range, then clawed his way upright using the side of the building as support. Then he, too, staggered off into the darkness.

Breathing hard, Bryce turned to the woman. She was in her forties, he guessed, smartly dressed and obviously frightened out of her wits. Speaking in French, he said gently, "It's all right, they won't bother you now."

"I didn't even hear them approaching," she quavered. "*Monsieur,* how can I thank you?"

"By allowing me to accompany you to your destination," he suggested. "And there's no need to thank me, it was my pleasure." He meant it, he realized, the adrenaline still racing through his veins. Routing two muggers was just what he'd needed.

Making small talk, he walked with her until they came to a more brightly lit street, where he left her at the doorway of her small hotel. Her profuse thanks already forgotten, he strode to his own hotel, nodded at the doorman and took the elevator to his suite. Entering it, he locked the door. Then he sank down on the leather chesterfield, his head in his hands. The little boy he'd once been had been unable to protect his mother; a rusty toy truck hadn't been enough. But tonight, putting the run on a couple of louts who'd been threatening an unknown woman, he felt as though he'd somehow made amends for that long-ago failure.

His mother would have forgiven his inability to protect her; indeed, would have seen nothing to forgive. Because Rose had loved him.

For the first time in thirty-two years, Bryce allowed that love to expand in his chest. To unfold like a rose, slowly and beautifully filling his heart.

Dimly he became aware that tears were running down his face, the difficult tears of a man who'd learned very young not to cry. His mother had been making plans to escape and take her son with her; to build a better life. Then she'd made her mistake: gone alone to the apartment, and found Fletcher waiting for her.

It was a mistake she'd paid for with her life. But of her courage and her love for her small son, Bryce had no doubt.

For a long time he stayed hunched over on the smooth leather, his chest shuddering with a grief he'd locked away years ago. Then, worn out, he fell into bed.

Because he'd forgotten to set his alarm, Bryce overslept. He felt like the one who'd been kicked on the cobblestones, he thought ruefully, heading straight for the shower. The hot water pummeled his aching muscles, and eventually cleared his head. If he didn't hurry, he'd miss his flight. Then it would be too late to phone Jenessa when he landed.

He made the flight with five minutes to spare, slept like a dead man most of the journey, and took a limo to his town house. Boston was baking under the afternoon sun; he was grateful for the shade of the tall trees as he ran up his front steps and into the air-conditioned cool of the foyer. Dumping his case by the door, he hurried to the phone. But after he'd punched in the numbers, he was met with an empty, repetitive ringing. Then Jenessa's voice mail clicked on.

He'd told her he'd phone on the weekend. This was only Friday. Bryce banged the receiver down. He didn't want to leave a message; he wanted to talk to her. Although, if he were honest, he still had no real idea what he was going to say.

Was that why he hadn't called her on his cell phone, earlier?

The need to see her, face to face, burned through his veins. He raced up to his bedroom, changed into casual cotton trousers and an open-necked shirt, then grabbed his car keys from the bureau.

He might well be going on a fool's errand. Sure, she could be out in the garden. Equally, she could be in California, making love to a surfer.

Did he really believe that? Did he honestly think Jenessa capable of so easily switching her affections from him to someone else, all within a week and a half?

He was still avoiding the word *love*. Yet wasn't her love as trustworthy as Rose's had been? Swearing under his breath, Bryce headed for the garage.

Focusing his attention on the road, he drove to Wellspring in record time; but when he walked into Jenessa's peaceful, sunlit garden, where carmine and white hollyhocks nodded in the breeze and dahlias stood like sentinels against the old stone wall, he found himself alone there. He climbed the back steps, knocked on the door and waited. Then he tried the door, which was, as usual, unlocked. "Jenessa?" he called. "It's Bryce—are you home?"

He was met with a silence overlaid by bird calls from the garden. Maybe she was in Boston, visiting Charles and Corinne. Or in New York with Leonora. He walked through into the kitchen, where, to his huge relief, he saw that she'd left a mug of coffee and a bunch of spinach on the counter.

A bunch of spinach—wilting spinach, at that—had the power to make him feel as though he'd been granted a reprieve?

Bryce looked around him. It was an unpretentious little house, surrounded by flowers and smelling faintly of oil paint. But didn't it hold all that he wanted? For it was home to a woman whose courage and integrity he'd come to trust absolutely; a woman who was creative, passionate and honest.

Jenessa. The woman he'd been waiting for all his life.

Because he loved her.

Somewhere a fly was buzzing against a windowpane. Bryce listened to it absently. He'd had to leave Jenessa, travel to a faraway city beside a river, and rescue an unknown woman from danger in order to free himself of the past and allow himself a future. A future to which Jenessa was pivotal. Essential. As necessary as the air he breathed.

As soon as she came back, he'd tell her that he loved her.

She must be somewhere nearby. On automatic pilot, Bryce wandered into the studio. The painting that had caused all the trouble was carelessly leaning against other canvasses on the floor; its certainties assailed him now, as they had then. As he shifted his gaze to the easel, he drew in a sharp breath.

The only certainty in this work was that there was no certainty. Nothing was to be trusted, love least of all.

It was an indictment of the way he'd lived his life. Even more strongly did it condemn the way he'd treated Jenessa, falling into her bed but rigidly refusing her an equal intimacy the rest of the time.

He could have lost her so easily; and it would have been no one's fault but his own.

Unable to stay in the same room with the painting, equally unable to sit still and wait for Jenessa to return, Bryce stepped outdoors again. He didn't want to stay in the garden either, so peaceful and full of color, scent and birdsong. Restlessly, he set off down the lane.

He'd walked for perhaps five minutes when he heard, carried on the breeze, the high-pitched shouts of children. Curious, he followed the sound, sighting through the trees a restored Colonial house surrounded by a large, untidy garden. In the apple orchard a long trestle table was set with colorful plates and napkins. The children, girls as well as boys, were playing a rowdy game of soccer in the field behind the house. Then his heart gave a great leap in his chest. Chasing after the ball, her hair flying in the wind, was Jenessa.

She was wearing shorts and a T-shirt, her breasts bouncing with her exertions. She appeared to be playing with very little regard for the rules, he thought, a smile tugging at his lips. But she was also making sure that everyone got a chance at the ball, from the littlest girl to the biggest boy. With no fuss whatsoever, Bryce fell a little more deeply in love.

How could he not love her? Generous, talented, fiery-tempered and passionate; kind and fun-loving; willing to change: all these were facets of the woman he'd probably loved since she'd hustled him out of her house before the christening, afraid that he'd recognize her.

If he were honest, she'd gained a foothold in his heart when she was only seventeen.

Into his mind dropped an image of that earlier, joyful painting. He was no longer remotely frightened by it because he understood it now: its fiery hues and deep knowledge were his as much as hers. He pushed open the gate in the white picket fence, closing it carefully behind him.

He was emerging from the orchard before Jenessa caught sight of him. She stumbled, tripped over a tussock of grass and rolled in a heap to the ground. In a few quick strides Bryce was at her side. "Sweetheart," he said urgently, "are you hurt?"

"What did you call me?" she gasped.

Her cheeks were flushed from running, her breast rising and falling under her thin shirt. Bryce said hoarsely, "Will you marry me?"

The soccer ball thumped her on the shoulder. Two little boys scurried up, one forking the ball away with his foot, the other yelling, "Sorry, Jen."

She said faintly, "You're the last of the romantics. Haven't you heard of candlelight and violins?"

"If you'll marry me, I'll light a bonfire and hire an orchestra," Bryce said, and waited for her reply. His breath was stuck in his throat; his heart was racing as though he was the one who'd been running the length of the field.

"Am I dreaming?" she said suspiciously. "Is this a case of classic wish fulfillment?"

"You're wide awake," he said, clasping her by the shoulders and lifting her to her feet. "I don't deserve you, I've been an unmitigated idiot, but I love you with all my heart. Today, tomorrow and always. Marry me, Jenessa. Please."

She jabbed her finger hard into his chest. "You feel real," she said. "Maybe you should kiss me. Then I'd know for sure."

As a chorus of yells from the far end of the field signaled a goal had been scored, Bryce bent his head and with all his newly found love kissed Jenessa until he had to come up for air. Against his mouth she muttered, "Yes."

"Yes what?"

She looked up, her eyes brilliant with joy. "Yes, you're real. Yes, I'll marry you. Even though it's been the worst ten days of my whole life."

"I'm sorry, my darling, more sorry than I can say. I can't even really explain it." Wrapping his arms around her so she couldn't possibly escape, he stumbled out a description of the mugging on a Paris street and the resulting brawl. "When I got back to the hotel, two things happened. I let myself feel all the grief for my mother that I've buried for years...but even more important, I realized how much I loved her, and how strongly she'd loved me. Somehow that freed me, in a way I still don't really understand.''

"It makes perfect sense to me," Jenessa interjected.

"As soon as I got home, I headed here," Bryce continued, "and when I saw that bunch of spinach on the counter, I knew. I just knew.''

"Spinach?"

"Yeah, spinach—don't ask." He grinned. "So I headed out to find you, and when I saw you playing soccer—breaking every rule in the book, I might add—I figured it was past time I got my priorities straight and asked you to marry me.''

"I don't quite understand what the spinach had to do with it, but I sure like the results," Jenessa said, running one finger down his cheek to the cleft in his chin. "You really do want to marry me?''

"As soon as possible."

"We'll have to invite Maybelline," she said.

"And Charles and Leonora and Samantha.''

"Samantha," Jenessa repeated, looking suddenly stricken. "I know I'm a raw beginner when it comes to babies, but I want to have one—yours and mine. Are you willing to have children? Or are you still afraid you won't be a good father?''

Two little girls in mud-stained party frocks ran up to them, panting and puffing. One of them tugged at the hem of Jenessa's shorts. "Jenessa, Keith won't let us have the ball...he's being really mean.''

"Okay, I'll be right there," Jenessa said, looking harassed. "You must tell me the truth, Bryce. It's important.''

The decision was already made, although again he couldn't have explained it to save his soul; he only knew that his fear of Fletcher's heritage had vanished. "Yes,"

Bryce said steadily, "I want children. We might even have two."

Her smile was radiant. "We could teach them to play soccer."

"I'll have to give you a rundown on the rules first," Bryce rejoined. "Let's go get the ball from Keith."

Three minutes later both he and Jenessa were embroiled in the game, to the imminent peril of his clean trousers and shirt. He'd been a star on the soccer team of the private school he and Travis had attended, and soon learned he hadn't lost any of his skill. But more than that, it didn't take three minutes for him to realize he was having a wonderful time; their future, his and Jenessa's, could be like this, he thought, kicking the ball to an angelic-faced little girl with a mean talent for dribbling.

From the sidelines, a whistle shrilled and a woman called, "Time out for hot dogs."

The game dissolved instantly. Jenessa smiled at Bryce, swiping her hair back from her forehead. "Come and meet my friend Susan. It's her son Max's birthday."

Susan was a pretty brunette with sparkling brown eyes. Jenessa said, linking her arm with Bryce's, "Susan, I'd like you to meet my fiancé, Bryce Laribee."

"Fiancé? Since when?"

"Since five minutes ago," Bryce laughed. "Here, let me help you with the barbecue."

"You're a dark horse, Jenessa," Susan chided, hugging her friend warmly, "this is the first I've heard about a fiancé. Bryce, the barbecue tongs are on the table and I'm delighted to meet you."

Bryce produced a large number of hot dogs, doled out chips and cans of pop, and gave up trying to remember all the children's names: perhaps because Jenessa was distracting him by feeding him a hot dog laced with yellow mustard, red ketchup and green relish. When she disappeared to get the cake that Wilma Lawson had made, he took the opportunity to follow her into the house and make a private phone call to the local florist, requesting immediate delivery of his order. Then he joined the others for ice cream and birthday cake.

An hour later the children had gone, Max and his brothers were playing amiably with some of the new toys, and Bryce was elbow deep in suds at the sink. He'd warmed to Susan immediately, and was amused at how skilfully she set about discovering if he was good enough to marry her friend Jenessa. It felt like an acclamation when she kissed him on the cheek as they left, promising to invite them both for dinner one evening the following week.

Arm in arm, Jenessa and Bryce strolled down the lane. Her bare legs were streaked with grass stains and mud, her hair a tangle of untidy curls; she was so beautiful he wondered if he could bear it. When they turned the corner and her house came in sight, she stood still, then threw back her head and began to laugh.

The florist had supplied bunches and bunches of balloons, all inscribed in big white letters, *I Love You.* They waved gently in the breeze, purple, red and blue, green, yellow, mauve and orange. Bryce said, "Couldn't see the sense of giving you flowers again, your garden's overflowing with them."

"All those colors," she chuckled, "what a perfect present for an artist. To think I said you weren't romantic."

"Once we get indoors," he said, his voice deepening, "I'll show you just how romantic I can be."

"How will you do that?" she asked, widening her eyes innocently. "By making a spinach salad?"

"Nope, that's for later. First I'll take you into the shower and scrub the mud off. Then we'll see what happens second."

Jenessa opened the front gate, passing between the bobbing balloons. "Bryce," she said, "have I told you yet today that I love you to distraction?"

"Not in so many words."

She smiled into his eyes. "I love you so much I feel as though I might burst, just like a balloon."

"Please don't do that," he said, smiling back. "I don't think I've ever been as happy as I am right now, Jenessa. Nor have you ever looked more beautiful."

"Wait a while," she said with the same innocent grin. "You might change your mind."

A couple of hours later, after they'd made love in her little bedroom, Bryce dropped a kiss on the tip of her nose and said huskily, "I adore you, and you are indeed amazingly and lusciously beautiful. But I'll always remember you standing in the lane coated in mud, laughing at balloons, your hair shining in the sunlight."

"You say the most wonderful things to me."

"Why don't we get up," he said lazily, "and phone the family? We could get married before Travis and Julie go to Mexico...would you be okay living in Boston most of the time?"

"Oh, yes," Jenessa said. "But I'd like to keep this house—it's where we met for the second time around."

"I love it here," he said. "It'll be a great place to retreat when the city gets too much."

"I don't want a big society wedding," she added. "Just a few close friends and family...perhaps we could have it here in Wellspring."

"We can do whatever you like," Bryce said, nuzzling her throat.

"I like that," she murmured. "Very much."

Another half hour passed before they managed to get out of bed. With Jenessa on the kitchen phone and Bryce using the phone in her studio, they called Charles. "Married?" he said, once Jenessa had told him the news. "You and Bryce? Congratulations, Jenessa! He's a fine man, and his business has done extremely well...I'm very happy for you. By the way, Travis and Julie are here, do you want to speak to them?"

When Travis came on the line, Jenessa could almost

see his smile. "Married, eh?" he said. "Best news I've heard all day. Took you long enough though...I was beginning to wonder if the two of you would get it together or not."

"Asking us to be godparents," Jenessa said darkly, "was it all a plot?"

"Who, me?"

"Yes, you, brother dear."

"If it was, I'll never admit it."

"I'm the luckiest woman alive," Jenessa said, "so I guess I'll forgive you. We're going to get married in the garden at Wellspring, and we might come and visit you in Mexico once you're settled in."

"You can baby-sit for us, Jen," Travis said. "Good practice."

As Jenessa blushed, Bryce interjected, "Don't rush us, Travis. I'm not quite used to the idea of the two of us, without adding a third."

"You're the guy who said at my wedding that the woman wasn't born who'd lead you to the altar."

"Seems to me I remember you saying something similar before you met Julie," Bryce remarked.

"Then we're both lucky to be proved wrong," Travis said.

And how could either Bryce or Jenessa disagree with that?

The world's bestselling romance series.

HARLEQUIN® *Presents*

Seduction and Passion Guaranteed!

OUTBACK KNIGHTS

Marriage is their mission!

From bad boys—to powerful,
passionate protectors!

Three tycoons from the Outback
rescue their brides-to-be....

**Coming soon in Harlequin Presents:
Emma Darcy's exciting new trilogy**

Meet Ric, Mitch and Johnny—once three Outback bad
boys, now rich and powerful men. But these sexy city
tycoons must return to the Outback to face a new
challenge: claiming their women as their brides!

**MAY 2004: THE OUTBACK MARRIAGE RANSOM #2391
JULY 2004: THE OUTBACK WEDDING TAKEOVER #2403
NOVEMBER 2004: THE OUTBACK BRIDAL RESCUE #2427**

*"Emma Darcy delivers a spicy love story...
a fiery conflict and a hot sensuality."
—Romantic Times*

Available wherever Harlequin books are sold.

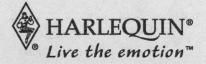

HARLEQUIN®
Live the emotion™

Visit us at www.eHarlequin.com   HPEDARCY

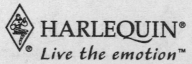

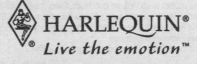

If you enjoyed what you just read,
then we've got an offer you can't resist!

Take 2 bestselling love stories FREE!

Plus get a FREE surprise gift!

Clip this page and mail it to Harlequin Reader Service®

IN U.S.A.
3010 Walden Ave.
P.O. Box 1867
Buffalo, N.Y. 14240-1867

IN CANADA
P.O. Box 609
Fort Erie, Ontario
L2A 5X3

YES! Please send me 2 free Harlequin Presents® novels and my free surprise gift. After receiving them, if I don't wish to receive anymore, I can return the shipping statement marked cancel. If I don't cancel, I will receive 6 brand-new novels every month, before they're available in stores! In the U.S.A., bill me at the bargain price of $3.57 plus 25¢ shipping & handling per book and applicable sales tax, if any*. In Canada, bill me at the bargain price of $4.24 plus 25¢ shipping & handling per book and applicable taxes**. That's the complete price and a savings of at least 10% off the cover prices—what a great deal! I understand that accepting the 2 free books and gift places me under no obligation ever to buy any books. I can always return a shipment and cancel at any time. Even if I never buy another book from Harlequin, the 2 free books and gift are mine to keep forever.

106 HDN DNTZ
306 HDN DNT2

Name _____ (PLEASE PRINT)

Address _____ Apt.#

City _____ State/Prov. _____ Zip/Postal Code

* Terms and prices subject to change without notice. Sales tax applicable in N.Y.
** Canadian residents will be charged applicable provincial taxes and GST.
All orders subject to approval. Offer limited to one per household and not valid to current Harlequin Presents® subscribers.
® are registered trademarks of Harlequin Enterprises Limited.

PRES02 ©2001 Harlequin Enterprises Limited

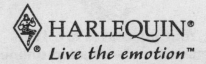